N3v3r!and

Nalle Windahl

First edition

Förlag: BoD – Books on Demand, Stockholm, Sverige
Tryck: BoD – Books on Demand, Norderstedt, Tyskland

ISBN: 978-91-7785-382-4

This book is meant for entertainment only. The organizations and operations are just a fiction of imagination.

Part I

Finding N3v3r!and

The beginning

I am going to begin where I will end. You need to wake up. It is time! You need to find and follow your white rabbit!

Now, for it all to make sense, you need to come full circle. So let's start from the beginning.

My name is M3rqrie, but that has not always been my name, it is my chosen name. I was born Anna. Grew up in an ordinary home, two parents, an annoying older brother, a cat and a dog. They are not part of this story, but for one aspect. I was always the little one, the one everybody needed to help. So frustrating. It alienated me and shaped me into who I am, an independent individual who can take care of myself and fix everything.

Early in my life I did not think much about everybody around me being either boys or girls. I just saw people. Most families contained one or two parents, and most of the families with two adults had a mother and a father, but not all. Some had two fathers or two mothers. By the time I was hitting puberty I had already discovered the love of my life. Computers. And as my body transformed from a girl to a woman, I kind of alienated myself from my body. It didn't feel right. And from the digital world, without really knowing that it actually was a thing, I saw myself as non binary. Both in the perspective that I am a human being, as in not digital, and that I do not consider myself either this or that. Not a zero, not a one. I simply am. Later in life, I realized that the whole sexuality thing was also something I could project my digital views on. A non binary binary person. Or bisexual as most people call it. I'm in it for the person, not the gender.

Now, from this you might think that this book is about sexual orientation and having a hard time growing up and being different. If that is what you expect, I am afraid I need to disappoint you. Hugely disappoint you. I only mention this because that is also another part of my childhood and growing up that made me different and strengthened my character as being able to take care of myself, developing into a lone wolf.

As for my name, M3rqrie, it is a mix between two of my childhood heros. Freddie Mercury (whom I share birthday with) and Marie Curie, who's enormous curiosity and intelligence I highly admire. Not to mention her bravery in the male dominated world of that time.

My path following my white rabbit

Well, now back to the path I want to show you, the path that will lead you to the end of this book. But before we continue. Have you seen the movie "The Matrix"? About a guy called Neo, following a white rabbit to find out the truth?

This path is my white rabbit, the path I needed to walk to find my truth. It is this path you will follow. This does not in any way mean that this will be your white rabbit. But I tell you this because I want to show you that it is possible for you to find your white rabbit, and it is possible for you to wake up.

Growing up with digital gadgets I have always been curious as to how they work, and why they work, leading me to experiment with every single thing I could get my hands on. Trying to make a thing designed for one thing actually performing another task that it was not designed for. One of my earliest memories is, unintentionally, attaching a microphone to the headphone jack and being totally terrified by the sound that came out of the microphone. Thought for sure that I had broken it. But I hadn't. Turns out it's just physics. Naturally, the next thing I tried was to connect headphones to the microphone jack, and to my surprise it worked that way as well, not that it was any good sound quality, but it worked. And on that path I have walked ever since.

The next gateway that I walked through was the digital world, through computers. Initially the computer was just a way to find information. Eventually it became the focus of my attention, wanting to know how it all worked and was connected. Gadget after gadget, function after function.

And at 27, before leaving the ordinary world and submerging underground, I already had about 17 years experience in the world of computers and various digital and electronic gadgets. My co-workers at the night shift in the security department of a big mall call me a gadget wizard. Mostly due to the fact that I built small gadgets for various purposes and tested them at the mall.

Sometimes they didn't work and I accidently set off the alarm, but since it was me and my co-workers that took care of the alarm, it was no big deal and no harm was done. Our little nightly secret. And they even started a betting pool where they were betting on the next date I would set off the alarm. To my relief I had already advanced my knowledge so much that it was rare that I triggered the alarm those days.

Online I am mostly unknown, I stay out of the spotlight, even the doubtful spotlight on the dark web. If you are not familiar with the dark web culture or social structure, I can briefly mention, without paying too much attention to it, that there are three arch-types of hackers. Whitehat, Greyhat and Blackhat. The Whitehats are those who use their knowledge to help build security to protect information and technology from being used by others other than those who own it and for their intended use only. The Whitehats stay within the borders of what is legal. The Blackhats on the other hand do not. They use their knowledge and other peoples technology for their own purposes. Leaving the Grayhats somewhere in between.

Again, I do not feel like I belong in either of the definitions above, I see myself as a no hat hacker.

Ok, I think that is about enough about me. I believe you have a sufficient picture of who I am and where I come from. This is not a story about me, and I do not want to draw the attention away from what I really want to tell you.

The secret organization

This is all about an organization called N3v3r!and and the network behind it.

Let's take it from the beginning. Or at least my beginning on this path, shown to me by my white rabbit.

At 13 I took my first dive from the internet down into the dark web. Horrified with what I found, I stayed out of it for almost a year, but my curiosity drove me back, like an iron ball is being pulled towards the magnet. Navigating around drugs, huge amounts of the worst possible porn, criminal activities and other more or less illegal stuff, I found a vast source of hack information that was simply not available on the internet. Now, the dark net being what the dark net is, it was like navigating a minefield, a rainy night, blindfolded, barefoot, cold, scared and dizzy. Not really the ideal environment for a 14 year old kid to be in. But I was fortunate. I found paths to follow. Not saying in any way that it was safe paths, but paths.

One of my first findings that triggered a curiosity that would lead me was, perhaps not surprisingly, a frame from a scene in the movie "The Matrix" after the main character Neo is told to follow the white rabbit, and the frame being when he lays eyes on it.

Now, perhaps you are thinking that a picture of a white rabbit might not be something special. And on any other day I might have agreed. But that day I thought it was strange that someone had gone through so much trouble having raised several layers of security around a small and simple storage area just to store a tiny image file with a frame from that movie. And not just any frame, the frame that sets Neo off into the first contact with events that would not only change his life but also change his entire view on reality and truth.

Call it instinct or childish stubbornness, but I knew there was something special with that image. Or perhaps rather, I wanted so badly that there would be something special with that image file. But it had to be something special. The location of the secret and heavy secure location was a back door on a server that is part of the digital silk road, typically one of the first things you find, or goto, on the dark web, as it is the biggest trading market for all sorts of drugs. Now, it is not unusual to find backdoors on servers, but this server in particular was reached through a tunnel called "the rabbit hole".

Which to me meant two things. It was another reference to the Matrix where Neo is said to tumble down the rabbit hole like Alice in Wonderland, making it even more credible as a carrier of some kind of important, hidden and secret message. And that the name was not selected by accident, it had a purpose.

It took me almost a year to find the hidden message encoded in the file. It was hard to find and even as I found it, I was not sure that I actually had found anything, it all seemed too random. But then again, it seemed to have been placed there deliberately.

I found nine characters in binary code. It translated to:

N3v3r!and

By then, I was already nerdy enough to be able to say something about it that would make me stick with it.

Computer nerds often replace letters with numbers, in this case the 3 could represent an E, making the first half of the characters *never*. The second half could simply be the logical statement of 'and', but not being true by setting the exclamation mark in front of it making it "*not and*" or it could be another replacement, even if it was nothing that I knew was widely accepted, but the exclamation mark could be a replacement of the letter "L".

Leaving me with either never-not-and or neverland. Neverland was familiar to me, from the Peter Pan story. Never-not-and was unfamiliar - but it was appealing somehow. Never. As in never gonna happen. Not and, a logical statement. Both this not being true and that not being true. If those conditions are met, it is true. Never both being not true is true.

Looking in the rear view mirror, I was too young to understand the complexity of it, and even now, years later, and with all the knowledge and experience I have, I still have trouble wrapping my mind around it, and I can still be amazed by the brilliance of it. A truly worthy opponent. Equally brilliant and dangerous.

An obsession

Needless to say, this hidden message became an obsession. I needed to find out more.

It took years before I found any mentioning of something that would cast a new light on my quest, and that would chase away any doubts that lay back in my mind, wondering if I made it all up, and that perhaps it was nothing more than a hacker prank, creating a tunnel called "the rabbit hole" and hiding a picture of a rabbit inside it… but that would not explain the hidden message in it.

But my next finding convinced me that it was real.

It was a document claimed to be stolen from a group of hackers that was said to have infiltrated various government and corporate systems, stealing secret information. The document in question was not really controversial, just a rotation schedule of the guards at the White House. Something that could easily be forged with a good amount of plausibility by watching the guards changes, noting time and routes. Just by being on site to observe and take notes. To make it more credible the document claimed to have the name of the guards, and the person who published claimed to have verified all the names as current employees in the security team.

But it was not the document itself, nor its content that sparked my devotion to find out more of what this was about. It was a file path stored in the metadata of the file, it pointed to a file server that was named N3v3r!and.

Of course, this was not proof in any way, but it convinced me that the N3v3r!and existed and that it was a group of people that was possible to find. I believed, correctly it turned out, that this odd combination of characters was not widely known and was unlikely to be forged or even added any value to the document or its authenticity.

What also puzzled me in the wake of this publication, was that the person who made the claim, and all the servers connected to the person all vanished from the dark web within a few days of the publication. Now, this was normal procedure by all means, precaution taken by several active users on the dark web to protect the true identity behind a username. Normally the user would pop back up with a new or similar identity, but in most cases they would want to keep their reputations from accomplishments made by one of their old aliases, so they tended to leak that information themselves. And this user was notorious for making claims to various things, including things that were not true.
But this time, the user did not pop up again, nor did anyone ever make claims on the accomplishments by that username or any known older aliases.

Rumors spread that this hacker had been shut down by the government, perhaps by some secret branch because of the implied sensitivity in the document. To this day, no one knows what happened. Not publicly anyway. I have a hunch of what might have happened, but I will not rush in advance.

Trader of secrets

By this time I had a big portfolio of tools and experience and a big chunk of confidence. I created an alias, again, not very uncommon, and advertised various services for payment. This is also not uncommon, but I never was interested in money, I was after information, thus my price was information regarding N3v3r!and. But. Why is there always a but? My gut feeling told me that this was not a good idea to advertise. Thus, my price was secrets. I requested information that was not available or widely known. This turned out to be brilliant in many ways, just not the way I had imagined. But eventually it led to my goal through a series of pieces of a very complex puzzle. I will not take you through all the steps, just the highlights and most important steps.

What I do share is that this alias shortly became widely known, which was unintended, but eventually became the final piece of the puzzle.

What I unexpectedly learned is that secrets tend to open doors that lead to new exciting places and opportunities. One of them being very unexpected, but very important in my continued search for N3v3r!and, was money. Even if I did not pursue money, some of the secrets provided plenty of money, without me actively needing to do something. Most often was the case that a target of the secret tracked it, offering big amounts to keep it a secret, and being involved in many secrets there was a big flow of money directed in my path.

Before I shut down the alias, I was even paid in advance if I was to receive a secret that I wasn't in possession of just yet.

This new found richness made it possible for me to drop off the grid for good, quitting my job, severing connections with the mortal world and entering the world in the shadows of the dark web.

The next clue

Next clue I got, which led me towards a more concrete path to search, was not information, but rather a theory from a client that offered it as payment for stealing corporate secrets from a world leading manufacturer in the food supply chain. The client claimed that all major food companies knew the bad effects of sugar in food, yet shamelessly spent big piles of money to develop cheaper substitutes to sugar, keeping the same addictive hook on the brain to make us buy more of their refined and artificial products, putting more money in their pocket.

The client got what he asked for, documents and reports showing what he already claimed to know, and in return provided me with a theory.

There was an organization, or group of people operating in the shadows of the dark web, just like me, that always covered their tracks, unlike me, but like me was interested in secrets and whose end goal was to bring down the current structure of economy and power. Their name was unknown but the few remaining tracks they left behind was an exclamation mark.

This suited the pieces I had already found and had connected to the N3v3r!and.

It opened a new door for me. A tricky path to follow. Do you know how many hits you will find in any search window of any platform containing whatever information if you search for an exclamation mark? Try it! Either you will get too many hits or none at all…

Again, this information was not something I thought I could, should or would share, because there is a fine line between searching for something on the dark web or being searched for on the dark web. There are plenty of knowledgeable people who do not wish to be found and go to great lengths to not being found. Should it be known that you search for something or someone that does not wish to be found, well, let's just remind you of what I told you about the hacker that published the document containing the guardrotation.

I realize that this probably sounds insane to you, but this is the path I chose, and is the life I have chosen. Whether it makes sense to you or not, I am comfortable with this life. Nonexisting in the shadows.

Next piece of the puzzle, believe it or not, was a recruitment ad. Not the common kind on a company webpage or on a social media page where you click a link, get to an application form that you can read about the job and fill in your information.

No, more subtle than that.

An altered image of Uncle Sam, with the text "I want you for U.S!" instead of "I want you for U.S. army". The colors of

Sam's clothes had also been altered and the stars removed entirely, but the colors were still blue, white and red, in that order from top to bottom. The same for the color of the text. This time there was also hidden code within the picture, but only a single character. The number 3.

The fact that the image again was hidden behind massive security and was only accessible through a series of tunnels leading to this one blind alley containing only this image made me strongly suspect it was the real deal.

Searches on the dark web revealed nothing to me that would give me any hint as to what this could mean, but I definitely connected the 3 to N3v3r!and.

Believe it or not, it was conventional searches on the open internet that gave me clues where to start looking next.

A search of the three colors, blue, white and red, in that order, pointed to the French flag, called "tricolore". Which to me confirmed to me that it was a solid clue, and an actual invitation to join the mysterious N3v3r!and.

France. That was where the clue pointed me. Now, France is a big country, and it is not much to go on, like finding a needle in a haystack, but I had managed to come this far, so I needed only to be patient and keep looking.

I covered much ground both on the internet and the dark web, without getting anywhere.

And in a desperate attempt I crossreferensed all possible connections with Neverland, Peter Pan and all the characters and places in that story in various combinations with France, Tricolore and areas and cities within the French border. But I only ended up with matches to Disneyland Paris.

It took me a while to realize that perhaps it was hidden in plain sight. Perhaps the reason everything was pointing to Disneyland Paris was because there's something there?

Going on a trip in the real world

I took a leap of faith as I booked a trip to Paris and a visit to Disneyland.

When arriving at the park, I had a pretty good idea of where to start looking, but no idea whatsoever what I was looking for. The obvious place to start was at the Peter Pan's flight attraction.

I stood in line, keeping an eye out for anything that might be a clue or a message. I took the ride, keeping an eye out for anything that might be a clue or a message. I exited the ride, still keeping an eye out for anything that might be a clue or a message. Nothing.

I repeated this two times. Still nothing.

By then I was frustrated. And a bit disappointed. I kind of thought it would be obvious and easy to find. A walk in the park, so to speak. Pun very much intended. But no, nothing. Nada. And my go to behavior to handle feelings like frustration and disappointment is sugar. So I set off to find ice cream.

While looking around I noticed that near the Pan attraction, there was Alice's curious labyrinth. Perhaps too much of a coincidence I thought, and headed straight towards it, only to enter and realize that I had not gotten the ice cream yet. Also typical of me, having one thing in mind, a task or something, then getting distracted by a stray thought and forgetting all about what I was about to do.

Well, I spent the next hours walking around this amazing maze. Still not coming closer to anything that remotely could count as finding a clue or message.

Exiting the maze I saw the Mad Hatter's tea cups and figured it was best to check them out as well. Still nothing and empty handed I was circling back towards the Pan attraction. The whole Alice in Wonderland track was perhaps just imagined by me, since the first reference to N3v3r!and was through the rabbit hole, which was both a reference to the Matrix, and to Alice in Wonderland.

With an ice cream in my hand, and outside Peter Pan's flight yet again I needed to clear my head and think. What could I possibly be looking for?

As I walked a bit away from the attraction out on a tiny bridge over some water I noticed a sticker on a streetlamp. It was a sticker of the Eiffel tower. What made me notice it was that the tower was turned upside down. And as I looked more closely at it, I realized that the tower was shaped as an exclamation mark. Not only that, the tower was colored in blue, white and red.

Again, a long shot, but my gut feeling said that this might just be what I was looking for, and since I already was in Paris, it was just a short trip to head back into the city and visit the tower.

Sightseeing in Paris

Said and done, about two hours after the ice cream on the bridge, I was looking out at the magnificent view over Paris from the top of the Eiffel tower. Again, not sure what I was looking for.

I circled the top floor a few times, looking at signs, searching for stickers, anything that seemed out of place. Hijacked several of the binoculars for longer periods to see if I could find anything through them, signs, letters, anything that would give me the next clue.

As I stood there I went through any references I could think of in movies, tv-series, books or songs that might be able to give me a hint to the next step. But I came up empty handed.

It had seemed so obvious when in the Disney park, the sticker clearly pointed to this tower.

The sun had started to set, but I still wasn't prepared to declare myself defeated. Not just yet anyway. I took the elevator down to the middle level and in frustration went around looking at every sign I could lay my eyes on. The only sign containing an exclamation mark was a sign inside a sealed off area and it was part of the warning sign to an electrical facility, possibly connected to the elevators. Either way there was no way I could get to it. As the sun set and the tower itself was lit up by hundreds of bright lights I felt my spirit drop along with the evening temperature and it started to get chilly.

Standing in line to the elevator to get back down, I noticed that someone had written something directly on the painted steel structure with a black marker. It was a heart with two letters in it. E and N I believe it was. Did not make sense at all, but sparked something new in me. I started to look around, and sure enough, I saw many places where people had left messages writing directly on the painted surface of the steel structure.

What if I had missed it on the top level? And now I was in the queue to get down to ground level.

Hungry and a bit cold, I decided to return the next day in daylight to examine the writing on the tower itself.

But back at the hotel I could not sleep, I just thought of what I might find, and if I would be able to decipher it if I found it. Patience is something I am normally blessed with, but in this case, I had none. I started to search the web for pictures taken at the Eiffel tower and zoomed in on the steel structure behind each and every smiling face, looking for writings. I kept at it all night, and just as I was about to quit searching and head down to grab some breakfast, I saw something in the background in a picture posted on someone's Instagram account. Barely readable in the light, and with a really shitty resolution of the picture, I could make out a series of numbers and above them the words: "The truth is !free".

That had to be it! I saved the photo for closer examination and headed down to eat breakfast. I needed sleep and energy. The allnighters I could pull when I was younger seemed far away, and even if I did not consider myself old, I was definitely not that young anymore.

After breakfast I took a warm shower and stretched out on the bed to close my eyes for a little while. But after an hour I woke up again, not feeling rested, but restless and eager to continue. I looked at the picture again, zooming in and trying to make out all the numbers.

It took a while, and a lot of guesswork and some processing of the image to get all the information out.

Truth is !free.
5129571400072923

The exclamation mark seemed to make it legit, again in two ways, their call sign and used to replace 'not', making the statement read "Truth is not free", which seemed to fit in with their agenda as well.

The big question was what the numbers were.

But before I started digging into them, I needed to get back to the tower to confirm that I had got all the numbers right.

Even with the picture to go on, it was hard to find the exact spot where it was taken, and finding the writing. But it checked out. I had gotten it right.

Cracking the code

Back home I started to work with the numbers. It was rather easy to exclude what it was not. It was not an IP-address. It was not a number cipher where letters had been replaced with numbers. Not even with Rot13. It did not match any registered phone number, not in France, not in any country that I could think of, nor in Peru, who has 51 as land code.

Still not sure what the numbers meant, I was even more convinced that I was on the right path and that the N3v3r!and was real. Of course they would not be easy to find. But to me, all doubts and questions whether they did exist or were a fabricated imagination were gone.

I just needed to figure this out, one step at the time. One riddle, one task, one challenge. Then the next, and the next.

For months I twisted and turned the numbers before I cracked it. And like before, when the secret was revealed I knew it was right. It made sense and the piece of the puzzle fitted nicely with the others.

Coordinates.

5129571400072923

Correctly spaced became:

51 29 57 14 00 07 29 23

And to follow the coordinate standard, there need to be two letters.

51 29 57 (14) 00 07 29 (23)

Just so happened that the letter N is the 14th letter in the alphabet and the letter W is the 23rd. So, adding every component of the coordinate standard it looks like this.

51°29′57″N 00°07′29″W

Now, where might that point you may ask yourself? Well, of course I will tell you.

It points to the Palace of Westminster.
This fits for various reasons. For one and two Peter Pan starts in London, and he flys past Big Ben. Reason three and four would be the attempt of Guy Fawkes to bring down the government, and the modern symbol of the mask that symbolizes Anonymous, the infamous hacker network.

Pieces that fit together, or are just a huge coincidence. But the latter is not something that I believe. Obviously.

Well, London it was, I had always wanted to go there, so why not? The only thing left to do was repack my bags for another trip.

Another trip

Felt like a tourist, going on one of those red buses, listening to the guided tour in headphones. Got a brief view of Big Ben and the Palace of Westminster. The brief look made me uneasy. An active building with high security arrangements 247. I kind of hoped that it would just be another sticker on a lamppost outside, but it seemed unlikely.

My first step would have to be to get inside somehow, and a quick search got me a way in, tickets to a guided tour that would begin in a few hours.

When the tour started I had a hard time concentrating on what the guide said, for two reasons. I was busy looking around, assessing the security, the technology, looking for anything that might be a clue, but most of all, I was distracted by the guide. A cute redhead with freckles. It is one of my weak spots. And she was really intoxicating.

It did not take long before I realized that this would be a tour that would not show me anything, and that I needed to gain access to the building somehow. Now, a common misperception is that hackers are primarily geeks with a vast amount of technical knowledge. It is partially true, but it is not the whole truth. The greatest trick the devil pulled was convincing the world he did not exist. One of the most effective hacker tools is interaction with another human being, with the goal to make the other person reveal things that they are unaware of. And even if my policy is never to mix business and pleasure, I figured, why not… after all, it is said that it is the exceptions that confirm the rule.

My mission object shifted in that instant. I paid full attention to our guide, and I even got her to blush a few times during the tour.

After the tour was done I approached her and laid a hand on her arm, thanked her for a very interesting tour and asked if there were any tours showing the lower levels of the Palace, more specifically the room where Guy Fawkes stored the explosives. As I talked to her I made sure to keep a playful eye contact with her the entire time, and did not remove my hand from her arm.

I am sure she felt the same tingling sensation I did, because somehow she agreed to meet me after her shift ended to grab something to eat and had almost promised me a private guided tour of the basement, even if she was not allowed to do so. She gave me instructions when and where to meet her, and as I walked out of the Westminster Palace I felt the familiar butterflies in my stomach and realized that this was probably the closest I would ever get to becoming James Bond.

Just to be sure, I took a few rounds back and forth circling the Palace, to see if I could find anything on the outside, kind of hoping I wouldn't, because I really wanted to get that private tour later on, having the excitement of the hunt a head, rather than already in possession of what I came to find.

Time passed slowley. And to my relief I did not find anything outside the building.

Private tour

When the time finally arrived, I felt like a child waiting for the first day of school to start. I was super excited.

As the guide exited where she said she would, I approached her with the same intense look in my eyes that I had used on her earlier.

I could tell she was both nervous and excited, and that made her unpredictable. And worse, uncontrollable. In a leap of faith I blocked her path, placing us face to face, really close, and playfully took a curl of her red hair and placed it behind her ear. I could feel her shiver, and the spark in her eyes told me that it was by pleasure.

I made an effort to get her to do the tour of the basement, and with much hesitation she agreed to do it. I thanked her with a quick kiss on her cheek, which made her face almost as red as her hair, but also sealed the deal.

I almost felt bad for taking advantage of this cute innocent creature. But I planned to get as much out of it as I possibly could, and give her fair compensation for her services.

To gain access to the basement, and not to attract too much attention, she guided me towards an entrance that faced away from the crowded areas around the palace, which suited just fine if I needed to come back here at a later time.

She took her magnetic card and swiped in the cardreader next to the door and entered her access code. My social hacking skills need much work, but I managed to get a quite good idea as to her access code, but I hoped I would get more chances to take a peak. And my wish was granted, we passed three more doors, of which one needed the access code to let us through. I memorized both the way and the code, just in case.

As we approached the room where Guy Fawkes had stored the explosives. I had to remind myself about the mission, because my private guide was really good at stealing my focus with her colorful description of what had happened down here on the 5th of November 1605. Both the events that led up to the situation and how it culminated in the arrest of Guy Fawkes that evening.

Just before we arrived at the door and she was about to swipe her card to open it, she surprised me by taking my head between her hands, pushed me against the wall and kissed me passionately. Then she took a step back and looked down at the floor as if she was ashamed or afraid, and expected me to get mad or something.

I pulled her close to me again and lifted her chin with my finger and whispered, "Do it again". So, she did, and the second time, she was even more passionate and by the end of our kiss she was looking straight into my eyes with a beautiful smile covering her entire face.

Apparently, she had only kissed boys before she kissed me. Which again gave me the upper hand. I could lead this in any direction I needed to. We held hands as she swiped her card and opened the door to the tiny basement room. To my surprise and disappointment, the room was empty. Nothing at all in it. I expected some kind of object or sign or writing that would contain the next clue. But it was totally clean. Not at all what I expected.

My guide picked up my disappointment and jokingly asked if I expected the explosives to still be there? She made me laugh, which was probably her intention. Then she continued to tell her story of what had happened there and a brief summary of all the events leading up to today.

Another clue

I thought I had hit a dead end, as this room did not reveal anything at all, but when we exited the room I saw something that I had missed when I was distracted with her kiss' before entering the room. On the opposite side of the corridor, the key word being opposite, was a door with a yellow triangular sign with a single exlamationmak in black in the middle of it.

A quick glance at the door and the closest surroundings told me that that door was not connected to the same system that gave access to all the other doors we had passed. It was an older keypad without a card slot, and from the looks of it it probably did not contain any near field communication device either. Just the number pad.

My options were limited. But the plan was obvious and simple. I needed to copy her keycard, and find the control system of that keypad. Copying the key card was the easiest part, I just needed to continue exploring this path with my newfound friend.

As we left I thanked her for an interesting tour and hoped that she still wanted to grab something to eat with me, but that I had one condition. No more talk about her work or the fascinating history of that place, just two people getting to know each other. She gladly agreed, without realizing that with the "getting to know each other" I really meant me getting to know her by giving her my full attention, plenty of flattery and getting her to where I needed her to be, to get what I wanted.

Now, finding a place to eat was not hard, there are plenty of good places in London, and since it was obvious that I was a tourist on a temporary visit in town, I let my new found friend choose a place. After about two hours, and a lot of talk and laughter, I made a move that I was sure to bear fruit.

I leaned over and asked her gently, if I was the first non binary she had ever kissed, and if there perhaps were more things that she wanted to explore with a non binary, and invited her back to my hotel room. As expected she accepted the invitation without hesitation.

Copying the keycard

I do not believe I need to be specific in what happened back there, but I will share the most important and relevant parts.

As she took a shower, I quickly made a copy of her key card. Now, perhaps you are doubtful as to how that was possible, did I really bring equipment with me for that purpose just in case?

The short answer to that question is both no and yes. No, I did not have any particular equipment with me, I had not planned for the use of any technical gadgets.

But also yes because copying a key card, or any other magnetic card for that matter, is much easier that you would think. For two reasons. The first reason is that the manufacturers need to let us merely humans know which card is which, and often, as in this case, the unique identity of the card is printed on it in plain numbers. So taking a picture of it is sufficient information to later encode a card with the same numbers as its magnetic identity.

The second option, which I also used, is to use the near field communication device in my phone to read the cards information, simply by holding it close to the back of my phone while an installed app gave me the full electronic identity of the card, which in this case was an extra layer of numbers not printed on the card.

Having this information stored, I could make a duplicate card with the same identity, and since I already had her access code from our visit, I now only needed to obtain some equipment to create the card and find the control system of the key pad.

Finding equipment is easy, at least for someone like me. There are a number of various, ordinary consumer gadgets that can easily be repurposed to perform new tasks. So a few hours after we had breakfast together, and I needed to let her go back to work, I had made a copy of her card.

Then I headed back towards the palace, almost feeling like a stalker, hoping she would not see me lurking around outside.

On a bench, with a large cup of coffee and some chocolate bars, I placed my computer on my knee and started to work.

The first and most obvious way to start was to see what I could learn from their wifi. But as expected, they had tight security around that, and I found no weakness that I could easily use to get in. But it gave me some information that I could continue to use to keep digging. Their public IP for communicating out on the internet for example. This led to their firewalls, and a few attacks on the firewall that any script kiddie could accomplish with simple premade tools like a hacker version of a swiss army knife, I knew the manufacturer and the software version of the firewall. This is good news to someone like me, because on the dark web, if you know

where to look or who to contact, there are plenty of weakness'
registered that you can take advantage of. This way hackers
can utilize the work performed by others, and not reinvent the
wheel each and every time. Saves the hacker community a ton
of time by sharing some information within the community.

A few hours later, several cups of coffee later, a big pile of
empty chocolate bar packings and inside a coffee-shop instead
of out in the open, I had swept through the entire network and
all connected equipment inside the building without finding
any trace of the system controlling the key pad.

Back at square one. No, not really, I had the key card and
access code. Just needed to find that last piece before going
back.

Review of the old clues

I returned to the clue from the Eiffel tower.

Perhaps it was 14 and 23 that was the access code on that key pad. Or, first or last numbers in the message? It did not seem to fit well into the bigger picture. There had to be something else.

 Not being too familiar with the British internet and phone infrastructures I thought it was best to head back to my hotel room for the final night before check out. Figured I needed more time to crack this, so in any case I needed to prolong my stay in London a few days.

I cursed myself for not planning enough time, but then remembered the wise words of Eisenhower; "plans are nothing, planning is everything". To me, this states the importance of making plans, and adapting them along the way, because a plan can rarely account for all possible events and outcomes along the way. Thus the need to continuesly reshape the plan as events unfold.

Back at the hotel I rebooked the flight home, and booked a different hotel for a few nights.

The last night at the first hotel, and using its public internet connection, I managed to dig around quite a bit, but also getting that IP blocked for intrusion attempts in several systems. Kind of felt sorry for the other guests that got blocked out of various services because of my laziness not to cover my tracks too hard. Just enough so it would not be traceable back to me or my computer.

A good way to spend the final night there. I could start fresh at the next hotel, with far more knowledge and a better picture of what I was up against.

Getting back into bed for a few hours of sleep I could smell the scent of my nightly guest from the night before. And for the first time in my life I felt alone, longing for companionship. But I knew that my choices would put any person I would welcome into my life possibly in harm's way, so I quickly pushed those thoughts and feelings out of my conscious mind.

Getting close to 30 I could understand why I had those thoughts and feelings, but they were not welcome. That was my choice.

Breakthrough

The next few days was again a search for a needle in a haystack, but the search paid off. Only to leave me feeling terrible stupid, and once again looking at the obvious.

An internet connection, unregistered, was assigned from a nearby connection-node. And on it, behind a firewall, a single server hosting software to control a keypad that controlled an electronic lock. The software was rather limited, and I could not do much, but I could easily find the existing code to the keypad. 0511. Remember, remember, the 5th of November. Why-oh-why didn't I think of that?

Well, with all the pieces of this puzzle, it was time to act.

I found my way back to the same entrance we used the last time, the card and access codes worked as they should and with a pounding heart I headed back towards the door on the opposite side of Guy Fawkes' room.

Luckily I did not run into anybody on the way in.

At the door, I entered the code, it was accepted, and I heard the click in the electronic lock revealing that the door opened.

As I entered I saw only a few things. A small table with a chair, and on the table was a tiny monitor and a keyboard. They were attached to an old computer which was only plugged into the power outlet, no other cables to it. I guessed that it was a stand-alone computer and that it would contain the next clue.

I sat down at the chair and hit space to see if the computer would wake up, it did and the tiny seven inch monitor revealed a terminal window with a prompt, nothing more.

As I started to type in various commands to explore the computer in front of me, I found a text file that was named "readme.txt". This was something that existed a lot, but normally nobody paid much attention to them, yet they somehow seemed to have survived and still to this day are common in various application folders. I am one of those who does not pay much attention to them, but since this was a hunt for the next clue, I figured I would actually read it.

The message

This is what it said:

Congratulations, you have entered our secret chamber. As you entered the code to get in here, you started a five minute countdown to set off the alarm in this building. It might be a good idea for you to hurry out.

Add your contact details in this file and save it.

Good luck!

Talk about an odd initiation ritual. But sure enough, I entered contact details to one of my anonymous front users and left the room.

I had almost reached the exit as the alarm went off. But I made it safely out before any security arrived at the scene.

I figured I needed to wait a long time before I was contacted, but to my surprise I had an email waiting for me when I got back to the hotel.

Front alias, where is the trust?

We've had our eyes on you for a while, and have a list of several of your accomplishments.

List ten of your best achievements, send them from your personal email. If you have at least nine out of ten, or we can confirm those claims we do not have listed, you will get the next set of instructions.

Naturally, I traced the email the message was sent from, but they had covered their tracks well, and I came up empty handed. As expected. When you are the one acting, you know in advance what you are about to do, and how to cover your tracks. When you react you are looking after clues that someone might have left behind, and again it is like looking for a needle in a haystack. Let's say there are a hundred ways to get to a certain spot. And on each of the hundred ways there are several options to use the way, walk, ride a bike, take a train, a bus or a car, run, heck, even ride a horse for that matter. Each way and each chosen means of transportation leaves various traces behind, and if you are the person to go to the place, you know which of the hundred ways you take, and which means of transportation you use. And to complicate it even further, you can take one way there, and another way back, also altering ways of transportation (which does not mean that there will be an actual digital horse left behind somewhere), and with that knowledge, it is easy to take actions to cover one's tracks. But when you look at that spot and need to determine how someone else got there and left, it gets a lot harder.

But as I said, I came up empty handed, and expected nothing less.

This situation made me nervous. I had no reason to doubt that they'd had their eyes on me, after all, I had been looking for them. But trust is a difficult thing, especially if you are asked to give it, without receiving it in return.

My initial reaction was to ask them for something in return, but I figured that even if I had gotten this far, I had not gained anything that would make me find them again. This was the closest that I had ever been, and perhaps the opportunity would be lost entirely if this door closed on me.

Perhaps this was not a time to get cold feet, or to think much, just act and follow the instructions. Didn't take me long to compose a list and send it.

The wait

Then time passed.

I came home from my London trip. I continued to live my life as I had done up to this point. But I felt uneasy. Restless.

The more time passed, the more I started to doubt that I would ever hear from them again.

But I couldn't help but to speculate as to what the next clue might be. My journey had started with a tiny clue to their existence. It had continued with a kind of recruitment ad that took me physically to two different locations in Paris, and then on to a physical location in London. It tested my skills as tracking down information, decrypting information, connecting the dots, and challenged my skills as a hacker, both in technical ways and social skills. It requested my total honesty. I had given it.

So, I could not in any way see that I would have failed the strange initiation ceremonies. From my point of view I had passed them all. With flying colors.

But I knew that it was not my opinion of the matter that counted, it was theirs.

Then, late one night. I got a message.

Unexpected request

Final test.
Black car, outside.
Now!

Without hesitation, I stood up, went to the door, grabbed my jacket and almost forgot to lock the door behind me as I was leaving my apartment.

Sure enough, there was a black car waiting outside my house. The back door closest to me was not entirely closed, I took a deep breath, opened it and jumped in.

The car started to drive as soon as I was safely inside. But I had to buckle up after it had started to move.

I could not see who was driving, because there was a solid wall that separated the back of the car with the driver's seat. The back of the car was entirely enclosed in black windows which barely let in light from the outside.

I looked around, I was alone, and there were no objects or anything else that revealed anything. Talk about a leap of faith. Should they wish they could easily kidnap me and make me disappear forever. After all, I had no idea who I was up against nor if they had good and peaceful intentions. I could only hope!

Since I could not change my current predicament in any way, I tried to relax and enjoy the ride as much as I possibly could. Even so, thoughts rushed through my head. It was not likely that this was their normal area of operations. This was my town, my territory, they probably would not know it as well as I could have done (if I ever left my apartment and got around to explore my surroundings).

And should I fail the test, they would need to cut all strings to this experience. Thus, I imagined that I would be taken to some kind of temporary arrangement. I would be surprised if they would show me the real deal at this stage.

The more my thoughts rushed around inside my head, the less scared I became. Sure, I was in a situation totally out of my controle, but I had no reason to be scared.

The car drove for about half an hour, and I was completely unaware of where I was. Probably more due to being totally unfamiliar with most of the parts in the city I lived in, rather than the driver disorienting me. There were various signs and landmarks that I could make out through darkness in the backseat.

In some kind of alley the driver stopped and waited. I was unsure of what to do and reached for the door to open it, but it was still locked.

Then, all of a sudden, one of the backdoor windows was opened just a tiny bit, and an envelope and a black cloth bag was shoved inside.

The envelope was in gold with a single exclamation mark on the back.

I opened it, and inside was a note.

This is your final test, but before that, you will get a choice.

After reading this message, you need to put the bag over your head. As you do, someone will open the door for you, and take you inside a door. Once the door is closed behind you, you may remove the bag.

The choices you have is to either turn around and walk out the same door you just came through.

If you choose that, we will let you be and you will never hear from us again.

Should you choose to go forward, there will be a door in front of you. Should you choose to enter that door, there is no turning back. You need to do what is requested of you. No questions asked.

Good luck, and remember…

...if you think happy thoughts you can fly!

To me, this was not much of a choice! Of course I would choose the door in front of me, and needless to say, I was very curious and a bit nervous as to what was waiting on the other side of that door.

The test

Again, without hesitation, I took the bag over my head, and almost instantaneously, I heard someone open the door, and felt a strong grip around my arm leading me out of the car, and along a staircase that had about five or six steps leading upward. It sounded like a metallic staircase, but I could not confirm it since I had the bag over my head. It was completely blocking out all visible impressions, not even shifts in light, if there were any.

I heard a door open, it also sounded metallic. Then I was led into a room, and as the door closed behind me, everything went completely quiet. No sounds whatsoever.
I slowly removed the bag and found myself standing in a little hallway with one door in front of me, and one behind me, just as the instructions had said. The small area was only lit by the low light emerging from the emergency exit signs above the door behind me. Like in a bad movie, it flashed every now and then, but unlike the movies, the blinking was not accompanied by the electric buzzing sound, it was completely silent. I took a deep breath and walked toward the door in front of me, and I slowly opened it.
On the other side was a corridor, and I could hear low voices up ahead.

As I moved forward in the corridor, the voices got stronger. I could not really make out what they were saying, but as I moved forward I could make out a few words…

…as you all know, we have somewhat controversial recruitment procedures, and with a little luck, we will shortly be joined by a very promising recruit, who has no idea what we have in store for her… but we are confident that she will deliver just what we ask her to do, and we believe that she will give a few things to consider after tonight…

My heart was pounding harder in my chest, as I kept moving forward, and I understood that it was me that the voice was talking about.

It sounded like a man, hard to say his age. But I was frustrated that he kept referring to me as *she* or *her…*

I arrived at an opening to something that looked like the side entrance of a stage area, the stage was lit with big light rigs, and there were microphone stands and cables along the scene. The backdrop was all black cloth and there were cables going back and forth in all directions behind the curtains.

I was so focused on what was up ahead, that I did not notice a person directly to my right who stopped me for a brief second, smiled at me, nodded and made a sign for me to continue forward.

"And here she is, our latest recruit… Welcome on stage, M3rqrie."

The improvisation

I took a deep breath, having a really hard time grasping what I just experienced. It felt like I was entering a mixture between a job interview and a talk show. As for the job interview, I had no trouble at all speaking for myself, but as for the talk show, I was not very comfortable talking in front of a group of people. But I figured that this might all be some kind of test. Besides, I knew I needed to do exactly what they asked me to do, no questions asked.

Thus, I took a deep breath and walked out towards the man. He was somewhere in his early fifties, tall, thin and with a white shirt, open collar and blue jeans. On his feet he had black leather boots, like a cowboy.

He turned towards me and signed me to come over to him in the spotlight.

He pointed towards a microphone and then turned out towards where the audience would be, but luckily, there was no audience, but there were a few cameramen with their camera rigs directed at the stage.

"Thank you for the introduction," I said looking at the man, "but I prefer if you refer to me as M3rqrie or 'they'..."

"Oh, sensitive, sorry about that, I was uncareful. I knew that, but it slipped my mind just now, won't happen again, I promise!"

"Thank you, and don't worry." I replied.

"You might wonder where you are and what this is all about. I will tell you." the man continued and made a gesture towards the cameras.

"What you see here is a live webinar with thousands of participants all over the globe, in various time zones. They are keen on hearing your perspective, as a hacker, on passwords and on social media platforms, especially from the point of view that someone like you might be interested in a person's social media account."

I had no way of telling if the man told the truth, that there in fact was a big audience online, or if it was just us in a room filled with tech and staff to make it look like it was a live online event. Either way, my task was to do what was asked of me, so I took a deep breath and started, something like this:

Most people do not consider passwords very important, nor do they appreciate the complexity demands most sites have with at least three categories of character, uppercase letters, lowercase letters, numbers and special signs. Nor do they appreciate the length of their password. Sure enough, best practice suggests a length of at least eight characters. And that is good news for someone like me.

Using a simple brute force algorithm I can find and crack an eight character password in about 1-2 minutes. Unless you are active on some kind of social media, in that case it may go a lot faster. And I come to why in a moment.

The first thing most people do wrong when choosing a password is that they use something that is easy to remember. Unfortunately, for you, not for me, a password that is easy to remember tends to be the same for many people, and, best of all, for me, they are widely known. You only need to do a quick search online on the internet and you'll find literally millions of hits. And this is only on the internet, that is without tapping into the collective knowledge of the dark web.

With a database compiled with the most common passwords found on the internet, we talk about seconds to crack your passwords.

With the collective knowledge of the dark web, we could be down to less than a second. Now why is that you might wonder? Well, over the years, hackers have obtained millions of usernames and passwords, to various known and unknown attacks on various sites. Should your username and/or email address be in one of those databases, it will most likely contain one or more passwords that you often use. Because sadly, it is a known fact that in order to easily remember one's password, most people use the same on multiple accounts. Which of course is good news for someone like me, saves a lot of time!

Now, as for social media accounts, they are a goldmine for my kind of people. Most people tend to use passwords that are easy to remember, which often include names of children, grandchildren or pets, favorite colors or flowers, a city you have a connection to, your favorite sports team and so on. This is information you are more than willing to share with the world online. But perhaps not the way you think. Sure, there are the innocent ways of posting a picture of a loved one or a pet, tag them and voila, we have access to a name and can possibly find a relationship between the two of you. Not that the relationship is important, the name of a person you tagg will still be added to the database and connected to you. But should a name be tagged with family or pet, then it is one of the first things that automated scripts will use when trying to bruteforce your account somewhere.

Add to this various 'tests' that you can do online, like 'find out what breakfast dish you are', vote on your favorite color, or pictures that circulate with something like 'let's light a candle for someone who is no longer with us. Share this picture and write the name of a person you wish you could give a hug, or an animal. All the answers you provide, are stored with your username and become a part of the common knowledge of the dark web. Available to those who are willing to pay for it, or traded, or in some cases, given away for free.

The best thing, as for passwords, is to choose a long password, at least 20 characters. Now, with that many characters, it is harder for someone like me to brute force it. Not impossible, just harder. It will be much more likely if you still are using words or names or colors that are tied to you in some way, like the things we can find out from your social media accounts.

But let's say you like Star Trek. In Star Trek there are various movies, series and characters. Let's say you mix and match a little and build a sentence of things that makes no sense, but is easy for you to remember.

It could be something like this:

7of9isnotfromVulcan!

That's a 21 character password for a Star Trek fan that consists of upper- and lowercase letters, numbers and a special sign.

I went quiet, since I did not have anything more to add.

Pushing for more

"Well, bravo!" the man said and applauded me. "You delivered well past my expectations! I hope our audience is paying attention, because this is something they really need to think about!"

He looked at me, as if he was waiting for me to answer, but I said nothing.

"Perhaps, if you would like to elaborate more and continue to educate our audience. What would you do, if a client came to you requesting secret corporate information?"

I stood quiet for a moment gathering my thoughts. If I was about to tell him, who I would suspect knew something about what I was capable of, or speaking to someone who needed to hear how to protect themselves simply by using longer passwords that are harder to crack, and not use the same password everywhere. I decided to go somewhere in between.

As a client approaches, they are often very specific as to what company they want to get information from, and most often they have a good idea of who's who in that company, but not always. Either way, my approach is the same. Gather information through the open internet, match with databases I already have access to, and if I am not successful, find some more databases, all depending on what kind of job it is.

Normally, I look for an IT-manager, who typically is trusted with a lot of access in the company IT infrastructure, but is perhaps not aware of all the risks and has easy to crack passwords. But it is usually true for low level IT-people as well, the ones that haven't got much experience and who never have been under an attack or having to clean up afterwards. Other high ranking bosses within the organization is also a top priority. And what most often does the trick is not attacking their work computer, but their private computers at home. Typically a child or some other family member. Or their own personal computer. In most cases, I find that the person in question has used private equipment to gain access to something stored on the inside of the company IT-infrastructure. In more difficult cases I need to place some kind of tracker program on a computer in the same network as the employee I am trying to get to, which often gives me exactly what I need to be able to penetrate a computer or a component in the IT-infrastructure.

"Well thank you, most entertaining. And I think that it is time to end this meeting. As usual, you all have ways to contact us for further information if you have any questions or want to know something more concerning any of the topics discussed here tonight. I hope to hear from you all soon, and see you next time!"

Seconds after the last word, the lights went out, and a voice called out in the dark.

From darkness to light

"We're out! Great work everybody!"

And then lights went back on, but not the lights that had been on during the event, but the normal lighting of the room that looked a lot like an ordinary movie theater.
The man on the stage was approached by staff that swarmed out from behind the stage. Noone paid any attention to me at first, but after a while, the man turned to me and walked over.

"Good speech! I was impressed, even if I had high expectations to begin with."

"Thanks, I guess!"

"Now, I would assume that you have about a million questions."

"About right."

"Well, M3rqrie, I will try to answer them all, in due time. For now, all you need to know is that you will be contacted again, in a more civil way than tonight. You've passed the initiation rite with flying colors."

"Thanks."

"I can not specify any timeframe, but expect to be contacted by phone, one of my coworkers will tell you what you need to know for the next step. The car that got you here is still waiting outside, just go back the way you came, and it will take you back home. That is all for tonight, thank you and good night!"

With those words, he turned his attention elsewhere, and no one else paid any attention to me, so I did as I was told, and headed back the way I came and as promised, the car was waiting for me and took me home.

Was it a dream?

I fell asleep almost immediately from exhaustion. And when I woke up, I was uncertain as to if it really had happened, or if it was just a dream.

I mean, it did not make much sense to be asked to talk about passwords and corporate hacking on a stage in front of an online audience. This was after all the N3v3r!and we were talking about, not your standard IT company. Not even an advanced IT company, this was a well hidden and very secret organization.

The next few days, I was back and forth between that and it was all just a strange dream, and that it really had taken place. I wished that I somehow had remembered to take the envelope or the letter with me, but I had no recollection of where I put it after having read it. I probably just left it on the seat next to me as I put the bag over my head. If it really had happened.

Then I decided to let it go. Should someone make contact I was ready, if it was just a dream, then I needed to leave it be. I would go crazy if I kept twisting and turning it over and over from every possible angle.

As faith would have it, just as I made that decision and started to feel good about it, my phone rang.

The phone call

On the other end there was a girl with a thick Scottish accent who introduced herself as Caren from something I heard as "bury it" (what a morbid name for a company I thought to myself). She said I was needed in London and her job was to book flight tickets and a hotel for the stay. She gathered a bunch of information from me and said that all details would come to my email shortly. But as we hung up I realized that she had not asked for it. But sure enough, shortly I got plane tickets and reservation at a fancy hotel in central London. A bit above my choice from my previous trip, but I was not complaining.

When I looked at the sender-domain of the email verification, I understood what the girl had said. Barrie IT. A company I had never heard of. According to its webpage it was a global IT company with offices in several major cities in most countries, the main office being in London. Founded by James Barrie in the 80's as a PR bureau, reformed over the years to an IT business with consultants in just about every aspect within IT. The name James Barrie sounded familiar somehow, but I could not place it. Yet it seemed to fit well with my recent experience. I was told that there was a large online crowd spread in various time zones.

The trip was scheduled the same day. What was it with these people? No patience at all! Well, nothing more to do than to pack whatever I could think of and head for the airport yet again, for the third time in a short while.

It was not until I was up in the air that I made the connection, obvious as everything else had been so far. James Barrie. Just so happened that the author of Peter Pan was named James Matthew Barrie. He was originally from Scotland but lived in London for most of his adult life. But he died in 1937, so I'm pretty sure it was not the same Barrie who founded this company. Most likely it was a corporate front for covert operations. That seemed to fit quite well with the bigger picture, except perhaps that the N3v3r!and I thought it existed was a small supersecret gathering of elite hackers, not a global company.

I was hoping the man on the stage was a man of his word, that I would get answers to all my questions. And hopefully now, on this week-long trip to London.

But at the same time, I did not want to get my hopes up too much, if this was just another step towards the end goal, whatever the end goal might be. At this point, with this organization, I did not take anything for granted.

The first meeting

When I arrived at the airport in London, to my surprise I found a taxi driver holding my name on a sign… he looked like he wasn't sure what to expect when holding the sign with "M3rqrie".

I approached him and said that it was me he was waiting for, he looked at me and asked if I was 'Em-three-Are-cue-rie', I just laughed and said yes, and then asked him if he knew where I was going?

He said of course: first to my hotel, wait while I drop off my luggage, then to the office building.

Fair enough, that was more information than I was blessed with.

When I got to the office building, I asked how much he wanted for the ride, but he just waved at me and said: prepaid, then drove off for his next assignment.

I stared at the building. More floors than I could count from the street, and the entire building seemed to be the Barrie IT headquarter. Very impressive. And you could see the Thempse river between the buildings across the street. Now, even if I did not know much about London or what was expensive or not, this seemed to be a very expensive location to have an entire building.

As I entered I saw a security desk and gates that all employees needed to pass to get through, first swipe an access card, then go through a manned security check with metal detectors and bag scanners, just like the airport, then another gate with access card. Impressive once again.

When I approached the desk the security guard behind the counter welcomed me with a smile and handed me a prepared envelope and said:

"M3rqrie, welcome. You are expected, go through the security gates and then take the elevators to your right. Top floor. You need to swipe your card in the elevator before you push the button."

Wow, impressed yet again, strike three. I did not have a chance to open my mouth before they knew who I was and where I was going. I would later learn how, but at that time, it was puzzling me.

In the envelope, among other things, I found a blank access card, all white. But I swiped it at the first gate and it swung open, and passing through security was no problem, nor the second gate.

The elevator had a marble floor and spotless mirrors. The buttons were black with different golden symbols instead of numbers, and as I pushed the top button nothing happened.

Then I remembered I had to swipe the card, and as I did and pushed the button again, a green light lit up the edges of the button and the doors closed behind me and started its way up. High level of security I thought to myself as I noticed two different cameras in the elevator.

The elevator moved smoothly and I almost did not feel when it started its journey upward, nor that it slowed down before opening its doors for me at my chosen destination.

The view that welcomed me was astounding. The London skyline was in front of me and I could see both the London bridge, the Millenium Eye and of course, Big Ben through the big panorama window that stretched from the black floor all the way up to the roof and as wide as I could see in the entrance hall.

There was no furniture and in the far end to the right there was a large black wooden door without handles marked only with a golden exclamation mark. That's my destination, I thought to myself and slowly walked over and knocked at the door.

It opened soundlessly and swung open inward revealing a dark room. Huge contrast from the sunlight area I was about to leave.

As I had entered the room, the door shut behind me, as silent as it had opened.

Total darkness.

Total silence.

Then, a tiny white dot of light, almost golden, ah, of course, could it be Tinker Bell approaching from a distance?

The introduction

Yes, it sure was, by now it seemed like the N3v3r!and was a bit predictable, yet, there was something entertaining about it.

Tinker Bell arrived at a large screen where she presented a sign out of her fairy dust.

Welcome to N3v3r!and

Then the room lit up and I saw three people in the far end of it. The man with cowboy boots, and two more unfamiliar faces.

Welcome to N3v3r!and M3rqrie!

Introduction may be in order.

We are the current core of this entire operation, I am P@nM@n, this is my second in command, H0kr and our right hand, TB311.

As you've probably figured out by now, you've entered this room through our corporate front Barrie IT.

Barrie IT is a legit global company with actual clients. But we are also a front operation for the secret network of N3v3r!and.

In general, with only a few exceptions, the employees of Barrie IT do not know about our existence, and that is how we prefer things to be. Just as we prefer that the outside world knows as little as possible about us.

You have proven yourself to us, and we would like to welcome you to our ranks. Our hope is that we may offer you a position in the company, and a place in our cause.

Naturally, it is hard for you to fully comprehend what all this is, and as for the position in the company, it may be a title of your choice, with either real or made up day to day tasks, depending on what suits you.

As for the cause, we believe a person with your brilliant mind and with your skills could contribute tremendously to us.

You are invited to us here for a week, for you to take a look around, at the company, at our covert bransch, ask questions, and look for answers. As said in the matrix, no one can be told what the N3v3r!and is, you need to see it for yourself.

Should you choose to accept the position, we hope you would consider moving to London, and of course we will assist in finding a suitable place to live. Should you choose to decline our offer, we part as friends. No hard feelings.

You have shown great trust in us, and now it is our turn to show you the same level of trust as we reveal ourselves to you, show you our real face and let you decide for yourself who and what we are.

As you might have heard on the webinar you spoke on, we have our own way of recruiting, and you are our first addition in five years. We are picky and do not want to invite just anyone. We take pride in doing things our own way, and from what we have seen from you so far, we are sure you will fit right in.

Part II

Exploring N3v3r!and

The overview

That first day, they showed me three things: an overview of the company and its organizational structure, and an overview of the organization behind N3v3r!and and finally, one of their most guarded secrets, a blueprint of their offline information databases.

Barrie IT was an impressive construct. Cells that operated individually and autonomously, no matter where in the world they were located. All units feed the central core which in return keeps each cell alive, independent of the economical result of the cell. Some cell's profit compensated the loss in others, with an overall positive economical balance.

If the construct of the company was impressive, it was nothing compared to the organization behind N3v3r!and!

A core of three people, the very same that welcomed me. Around them, three individually operating cells without connection to one another. Only connection to the core. Outside each cell, other cells emerged, each independant and only connecting to the one directly above it, and to two beneath it, giving each cell three connections. A holy Trinity.

How vast the cell network was spreading, I had no idea, but the basics of it were brilliant. Compartmentalizing every piece of information, operation and resource. Keeping every area of communication clean and controlled with strict protocols.

Should one cell fall, there were autonom reconnection protocols that made new connections between cells, so each cell always had one cell above it, and two beneath it. Like a beehive the center was protected by the surrounding cells, and it was most unlikely that the beequeen, or the core team, would ever be compromised. If that happened, almost every other cell in the entire organism would have already fallen, leaving the network crippled either way. It was not outspoken, but I suspected that in case of those events, there were backup protocols that would ensure the survival of N3v3r!and but in a different shape and with different individuals.

I was told that if I accepted to be a part of the N3v3r!and, I would be a nowise at first (something I assumed was a pun on the word novice, but also insinuating that I was not wise as of yet), and that I in time would connect to become a cell somewhere in the hierarchy, depending on my choices. It made kind of sense, but did not give me any clues as to what lay up ahead for me.

The third and perhaps most impressive thing they showed me was the blueprint of the heart in the N3v3r!and, their information library, nicknamed the JR. They explained that this was the true core of the entire operation, Joint Research. It was a physical, secret location where individuals of the N3v3r!and could contribute with information and take part in information provided by others. The setup was rather clean, an entrance where you could drop off information, with no access to the already stored information. And another physical access point where you could read the already stored information, but no way of altering it or extracting it. Yet again compartmentalized.

After this, my first day was to an end and I was asked to return the next day.

The soundtrack

That night I caught the light of the setting sun and welcomed the dark sky and its millions of stars on a bench by the Thames with the latest release of one of my favorite artists Muddhedd. Just out was the EP "Wild Oak". Without knowing it, this would be the soundtrack of this whole experience. At first "High on life" led to a sensation of being "New-born". Eventually "Fading" and "After Darkness" became "Wild Oak" in the vast forest of oaks. It is wild that Muddhedd just assembles a bunch of sounds in harmonies and rhythms and viola - a song… there is indeed something "Playful" with it (which just happens to be another release of Muddhedd). Sorry about that, just playing with words, an old habit I inherited from my father. But that night truly felt, and later turned out to be, a life changing moment. It just wasn't the change I initially thought it would be. That night I had already decided to accept the offer to join, but I was still uncertain about if I would like to have a "real job" at the Barrie IT company, or just being employed there to get a paycheck.

The next day, after a good night's sleep in the fancy hotel, and a wonderful, huge breakfast, I was back at the office building. This time I was greeted at the guards by the desk once again.

"Good morning M3rqrie! You are expected at Shield".

At Shield? As in the Marvel movies? Who was I meeting today? Nick Fury himself?

The guard must have seen the puzzled expression on my face.

"The elevator buttons, swipe your card and look for the one with a shield."

With the same procedure as the day before, I passed through the security gates and headed for the elevator, after swiping my card I looked for the Shield symbol, uncertain if it was an actual shield or the eagle that was the symbol for shield in the Marvel universe. Turned out to be the regular shield, and I was a bit disappointed, kind of hoping for the other.

On the Shield-floor I was greeted by an employee who was tasked to show me around. This was the IT-security department. It was a young guy, who obviously did not believe that I knew anything about anything technical, he explained everything to me as if I was a child. So it was great pleasure to see his reaction when we got to the part where he, according to his instructions, led me to a computer and provided me with my username and password. It took me just a few minutes to get a clear view of the internal IT-infrastructure and also figure out how the guards knew how to greet me by name. Cameras everywhere, with advanced face recognition software. Probably linked with the visitor list and/or a CRM, possibly even the employee database.

The poor kid did not understand what I was doing, it felt like he had never seen the terminal window, nor knew the power it contained in the hands of someone like me… He went totally quiet and did not say much for the rest of the day, and I resisted the temptation to explain to him what I was doing, but I figured that he probably had not been briefed about who he was guiding, so I could not really blame him…

One fascinating thing about the corporate network setup, it was also built in independant cells, if one network failed or was attacked somehow, it did not affect the other functions or cells at all. Seemed to be a reoccurring theme and most likely something that was considered a big strength, which of course meant that this was a weakness that could be used. Not that I at the time would think of any reason to use this knowledge.

What I did not find, which was a bit disappointing, was a customer database or CRM. And I was not prepared to ask my chepperon if he knew anything about it, I just noted it and saved the question for later.

Since I was not granted any administrator rights in any systems nor the network itself, this was of course one of the things I granted myself right away. I would not accept working in a place without full access to everything.

That evening was a rerun of the previous, except for the songs on my playlist, that evening was a mix of Red Hot Chili

Peppers, Michael Jackson and Queen - and of course, Freddie Mercury. It felt surreal to be in London, and finding N3v3r!and, and on top of that, being offered a position there… not that I was not worth it or could deliver and contribute, just surreal. On one hand, it felt like this is what I was meant to do, that everything I had done up to this point in my life was leading to exactly this moment. On the other hand it felt too good to be real. I guess in hindsight, both feelings, even if they felt conflicting at the time, were correct.

The third day

Third day was the most exciting. For many reasons. The first thing, and it struck me as odd at first, was that I was meeting P@nm@n at a café for a long brunch session. I figured that if this was the corporate culture, I would soon be needing a new wardrobe with at least two sizes up. But then again, I could also take the opportunity to adopt new habits. Turned out that I didn't need to pursue new habits nor buy new clothes, I managed to keep a balance anyway.

We discussed a lot, rather than P@nm@n informing me of things. He presented me with a lot of views, which I will recite later, but the entire day led up to one critical moment, which he did not push for, but let me discover by myself. Nearby, in the Thames, there lay an old boat. Seemed to have been there for ages, a familiar sight along the river. But unlike many of the other boats, this did not seem to be in active use, nor an attraction for tourists. It just seemed to be anchored there, stationary for the purpose of just being there. The name of the boat was Happy Roger. I thought this to be an odd name, since most boats are named with female names, but at first I did not think more of it. Only moments later it occured to me; another word for Happy would be Jolly, and if the boat was named Jolly Roger, it would be a pirate ship, and not just any pirate ship, it would be the ship of Captain Hook. At this point I had stopped believing in coincidences when it came to N3v3r!and, so I did not figure that I needed to ask, I just circled back to the boat and entered it, with P@nm@n accompanying me… He didn't say a word, but when I saw the cardreader of the first door we encountered, I figured I was on the right track and swept my card. Access granted. Inside was a tiny room, three screens with keyboards and USB-slots.

P@nm@n explained that this was the drop off point for N3v3r!and offline information archive. Each drop off point was a simple terminal, cleanly reinstalled between every use, to prohibit any malicious code from running and possibly infecting the environment. Another layer of the security, oh what a brilliant layer, was that the only information that was allowed in was plain text, leaving minimal risk of exposing the system to code. P@nm@n claimed to not knowing the specifics, but that the information flow was something like logging in to the terminal, attaching the USB-drive, then an automatic copy of the information started, and was washed through several processes to ensure no code was inserted, then indexed, flagged and tagged and uploaded to the general database. The only downside with this heavy security arrangement was that it was hard to get people to update information since they needed to physically go here… also accessing the information for the same reason, but it was a necessary security arrangement for the time being.

Speaking of accessing the information, that was the next thing, P@nm@n took me to the lower levels of the Happy Roger and showed me an access terminal. It was the same basic principle, except that these terminals did not have any usb-ports, and the screens were not screens, but a kind of glasses that presented altering information in high frequency and alternating between the left and the right eye, so that our eyes could read it, but not any known camera equipment.

And the user interface of accessing the information was super simple, command line based and asking simple search string questions, like an old wiki but in Dos-environment. As soon as the terminal booted up, this also a fresh installation each time it starts, you need to login with your user credentials, and then you only get to access the information, no other possibilities from the prompt, and no way of getting below the hood, at least in theory, because as a hacker I know there is always a way, except that even if there was a way, it would only reveal what I already knew, an offline simple database, without any access to or from the network. At least that was what I was led to believe at my first visit. Later I would find out a great deal more, but let's not move in advance, but let's just say that they were covered if something were to happen to the location or the location itself were compromised.

Now, accessing information, that was interesting. Imagine each and every conspiracy theory, mixed with legends worthy of Atlantis and King Arthur himself, and give that steroids, now you are getting close to the information found in this database. This and every dirty piece of information on every thinkable individual that ever held a position in the public sphere. Tabloids would probably explode if they would get access to this information, and Wikileaks seemed like a child's storybook compared to this.

P@nm@n explained that their view was that truth is a perspective, one man's guardian angel is another man's slaying demon. Thus, each and every single piece of information in this database needed to be viewed in the right perspective. But, the nice thing was, information from one perspective, used from a different perspective, could lead to unexpected outcomes. That was the true power of this database.

To me, it seemed like fiction and fact was mixed with fantasy, conspiracy and hoaxes. Spanning from UFO's and aliens, the JFK murder, 9/11, Area 51, Elvis-theories, Illuminate, FreeMasons, church, politics, politicians, nations, economics, and historic events and its purpose and possible connection to recent events. Typing in any keyword resulted in loads of hits, and combining keywords, which normally is a good way to reduce the number of hits, almost seemed to increase the number of hits instead.

The trick, I learned, was to write spiders crawling through the information to compile a reasonable amount of hits.

Later, I would spend a great deal of my time here, doing research. And yes, like most people who google themselves every now and then to see what comes up, I did the same in this database. And wow! I almost felt like a celebrity! Again facts and fiction, mixed with baseless rumors and partly accurate information. Like my own gossip channel. Creepy how someone, or perhaps several people, have had their eyes on me and tracked me. Well, that's it folks, what you do on the web, internet or dark web, may always catch someone's interest, and you'll never know what information someone might gather on you! Not even if you are as careful as I am! And it is no guarantee that they will get the information right either.

The Batman and the second date

At the end of day three P@nm@n asked me to take a day to gather my thoughts and come back to the office on the fifth day for a final dialogue regarding the way forward. When I was about to protest and say that I'd already made up my mind, he hushed me and said that this was protocol, whether I liked it or not. So, on the evening of the third day, I decided to catch a movie, and where better to catch a movie in London than at the Odeon cinema? The Batman was the most obvious choice, and I kind of smiled to myself thinking about what I was about to do, kind of like Batman, one identity in public, and another in the dark.

I don't know if it was being in an unfamiliar place, but normally when going to the movies alone, I enjoy the experience, but that evening I felt lonely. This probably led up to the decision on what to do on day four. My day to think.

I did not know anyone in London, except my one-nighter from the previous visit, so I figured that I would pay her a visit at work. Of course, it was not hard finding out if she worked, I knew my way around their security system, and could see that she had used her access card that day.

When I got there, I figured that this could be awkward, but still I wanted to see her again. Even if it would only be for a brief moment. But it was a happy reunion. We decided to go on a second date that evening.

A nice dinner and a walk through a London that showed itself in a cold spring, post covid suite. Intoxicating. Perhaps it was my sweet company, perhaps it was the entire situation, but I was genuinely happy. Again, things heated up between us and we headed back to my fancy hotel room. She was impressed with it, and I ended up explaining the entire situation (the official story) to her, a job interview with the company paying for the stay. Of course she was thrilled that I might be moving to London, and urged me to accept it if I was offered the position. She even offered to help in finding somewhere to stay, because the housing situation in London is what it is. The next morning, after a nice breakfast and a lot of cuddling, we said goodbye once more, but this time I got her number, and she asked me to keep her updated on the progress. I was thrilled about it! Figured that this new life in London would be a welcome break to my lonely life back home. Self chosen, but still lonely from time to time. Now, I felt a longing to belong. To have a place and a context. Be a part of something. Matter to someone. Take my place in this world, even if I knew I would still lurk around in the darkness and the shadows, but it could be possible that the shadow and darkness would not be my entire world. For the first time since I could ever remember, I felt hope and joy. And being active in the N3v3r!and could possibly, at least I was hoping it would, be part of something that really mattered and making a real difference in the world. Sadly I was right, but for the wrong reasons.

High on life (Muddhedd)

The last day at the office was almost a celebration. I was sent up to the top floor again, this time the room was not dark, but light, and when I said I wanted in they brought out champagne, balloons and a big pile of paperwork to be filled in.

I could not believe it, but I got both a big fat salary and an apartment in London, not a big or fancy apartment, but still an apartment. About 25 minutes walking distance from the office, which was unbelievable, considering it being in London. But it suited just fine! I was handed the keys right there and then. Another benefit was a gym membership at a gym not far from the office building.

I had decided on a bullshit working title and no official tasks, but said that I still wanted to contribute in the ways I could, both to the company and the operation. It was welcomed in all aspects, and the ideas I presented at the table were also encouraged. They offered two last things as onboarding bonuses. Help with arranging the move to London and a cab ride from the office to my new apartment including a 30 minute stay, then directly to the airport to my plane back home. Or rather, what would soon be my former home.

I got a week to prepare the move and then I would start with a few days of corporate training, followed by operation training.

I was really excited and was eagerly looking forward to both training sessions.

My new apartment was indeed tiny, but I figured that I did not have that many things, but I was thinking that I would bring my bed, get rid of the rest of the furniture and buy new when I got here. A sofa and a big screen TV. A small kitchen table for two with comfortable chairs. And of course a desk with room for a few screens and my computer riggs. The apartment was located in an area that seemed really cozy. A convenient store just around the corner, and the tube just a block away. This was a really nice place to build a new life.

Back home, it felt like I had left a modern movie, not only in bright color in high resolution and framerate, but with the latest animation technology and camera equipment, worthy of the most expensive movie production, and getting back to a black and white silent movie with Charlie Chaplin. My old life seemed pale in comparison to what was awaiting me in London. I really badly wanted to text.. hmm, I should give her a name, because I do not want to use her real name, so let's use Bella, as in Bella Reál, a new character in the Batman that was introduced in the movie I just had watched, just as she was a new character in my life, and certainly a character that was very real, and kept me real throughout the events that followed. And as I was saying, I was eager to text Bella, but I figured I needed to get a local number in the UK, so I decided to wait until then.

It was not hard packing up and leaving this dull life in black and white, and looking forward to the new life in HD color. It was like a week of vacuum just waiting. Thoughts about my future running wild in my head, developing my ideas as to how I would be able to contribute.

New-born (Muddhedd)

And like that, I was in my new apartment, the day before I was staring at the Barrie IT company, with two weeks of unreal blur behind me, and with lovely Bella helping me unpack. She even brought flowers as a housewarming gift. Now, this book is not a love story of my life, and the entire reason for mentioning Bella will hopefully be clear later on, but for now, I will leave her out of the story, with your knowledge that up to this point, she had play important parts in taking me this far on the journey, and that she would keep me company further down the road. Naturally, I came clean with her, not leaving any part out, because I would not like to build my new life on lies. And I was lucky that she both accepted me and my background, and forgave me for using her the first time we met, even if she repeatedly claimed that it was she who had picked me up and made moves on me, and not the other way around. Her presence in my life was an anchor and a beacon of truth and the good in the world. My sugarcoating in life. See, it's hard for me to stop writing about her, even now.

Then it was time for onboarding in the company. Official Training Day(s), but nothing like the Denzel Washington movie. Luckily. It was a typical corporate presentation, the structure, financial information, business models, client segments, support organization, internal support organization, facilities, traveling possibilities and how and what to do if work was needed in other offices in other countries.

What made the most impression, and stuck with me, was the type of clients. Spanning from private citizens, rich and famous, totally unknown, to persons with high profiles in the corporate world, politics and other organizations. But it did not stop there. Various high profile corporations and organizations were represented as clients, along with governments and other important structures within many countries. High profiles to nobodies across the entire spectrum of just about everything in the world, and across the globe. Impressive customer base. Adding to the oddity about it was that the company strategy was no advertising and no official positioning, only recruiting customers on recommendations from others. Which explained why I had never heard about them before I started work here. Also, another thing that was contributing to this was the many different front companies, sometimes several within a country, that represented Barrie IT locally, through a partner program, but without any public connection to Barrie IT. Brilliant setup if you wanted to keep a low profile as a company, which evidently was core business for this company. From what I could tell, it was not clear even to most clients that they were clients to Barrie IT. Except for one special client segment, in the beginning, unclear what made these different, but there was a core client segment that indeed was clearly connected to Barrie IT. Took me a while to piece out what separated this segment from the others, but as I did, I realized that it was this segment I had spoken to when I was "initiated". This realization stayed with me for a while, nagging in the background, but it was a piece I could not fit at the beginning.

Next step in onboarding was the initiation in the N3v3r!and. Now, I do not know how boy-clubs like the Freemasons or Illuminati, or whatever, have their initiation rites, but I am pretty sure that they are nothing similar to what I experienced. Where I expect that the boy-clubs have a live theatrical experience, this was all digital. A kind of movie experience. Again I was taken to the top floor and the room with the exclamation mark… All dark, with a single chair in front of the big screen that made up the entire wall on one side.

At first, total darkness. Then a tiny dot of light, far away, slowly getting closer. And a deep voice out of nowhere: "At first, there was nothing, then boom…" there was a soundless explosion in front of me, and then the entire universe was displayed, "…there was everything…"
Then a rapid journey through galaxies and stars before everything stopped just in front of earth. The experience made it tickle in my stomach as if I was really moving physically, which I knew I wasn't, but it didn't matter to my brain at the time.
Then earth just sat there, spinning slowly to a peaceful tune. It was a prehistoric version of earth, now I am not an expert on geology or something, but it looked like the continents slowly formed and I could see the planet changing over time.
Then it was time for another zoom, and a new tickling sensation in my stomach. It was a scene where some cavemen

were gathered around a fire. The crackles from the fire were clear above the peaceful music, but suddenly it changed and became louder and more dramatic. The crackles were no longer hearable, and in its place there were roaring, distant screams and sounds of fighting. The people around the fire rose to their feet, some fled away from the sound, some stormed towards it. Everything faded to black, but the sound continued, and it was clear that the people I just saw were attacked by other people, and it did not go very well. I was relieved that I didn't have to watch it happen, it was enough just hearing it.

The music changed in amplitude, tempo and mood and became slow and sad.

Then there was a text appearing over the screen.

"People have always worked together to create, to survive, to build, to thrive. What is created by some is desired by others, and what is taken by some is lost by others. The strong take what they want, when they want, the violent opress whoever they want, when they want. The world is not just, it never was."

Then images and scenes flash by of historic events, showing people working together, devastation caused by humanity, individual achievements, individual tragedies. Competition. Envy. Destruction.

Made me think that humanity is certainly not at its best, not in history, not now.

Then another text.

"Governments formed, laws were created. Order was established. Order was threatened. Order was upheld and

reinforced. The world developed. Order faced a new threat. Order adapted. Survived. Until today…"

Then everything was black again. A new song, powerful and upbeat and a text barely visible in the dark, almost like it was hidden behind some kind of mist or smoke:

"Welcome to the new world order!"

Then an exclamation mark in gold appeared. And around it, after a while 'N3v3r' on one side and 'and' on the other.

Then text again, flowing upwards and into outer space like the Star Wars intro:

"Governments are in control of law and order. They watch us. They control us. But who watches them? What keeps the governments to honor the people who elected them? What prevents power from corrupting power? Keeping power? Staying in power? Who watches out for the individual, for truth, for justice? When individuals reach power, they become power, and they will not let it go voluntarily. They make sure to stay in power. If not in public, behind the scenes. They make arrangements to keep the power. They have formed a subculture behind the governments. A world of power in the shadows. The governments are fronts. The corporations are fronts. Wars are a front. Pandemics are a front. They rule with economics and fear as their primary tool. A scared population is easy to control. A population in debt will fall in line. Those who have something are afraid to lose it, and they can make you lose it, they control your fear. They control you. We take pride in watching the watchers, we take pride in directing the spotlight and lighting up the shadows. We put fear in those who control you.

We are N3v3r!and!"
Then all faded to black again.

Naturally, it is hard to reproduce the entire experience, but to
the best of my ability, that is what happened. Perhaps not
exact wording, but close enough. At least the point of it, even
if I suspect it was more elaborate and well phrased than what I
can give you.

Then, just like in the movie theater, the lights came on, slowly
fading up to reveal the room, but not bright enough to pierce
your eyes. Then the three entered the room and placed
themselves in front of me, standing with P@nm@n and H0kr
directly next to me, and TB311 a little behind them, forming a
human triangle with the point away from me.

They did not say anything, just signed for me to stand up. As I
did, I was blindfolded. And by now I knew that it was all
theatrical and was not the slightest affected by it.

Seeing the heart

They led me out of the room, to the elevator. One of them swept their card and we took a ride to an unknown floor. The elevator ride felt long, but I was unsure if it was because I could not see anything, or if it was the silence or something else that made it seem to go on forever.

When we got out of the elevator I was told to stand still and wait.

I could hear familiar sounds of spinning fans, but more powerful, probably from servers in a server hall or something like that, and the sound of footsteps as the others left me. Then nothing for a while, except the fans. Suddenly I heard the voice of P@nm@n, but from loudspeakers. He instructed me to take one step forward. And then another. Then turn to my right. Then a few more steps forward, I don't remember how many.

I was instructed to reach for a door handle and open the door. I had to feel my way around before I even found the door in front of me, and it took a while to locate the door handle and open it. The door was heavy and I was unsure if it opened towards me or from me. At first it did not move in any direction, but as I pulled harder it opened towards me, and I could feel the air getting colder, much colder, and the noise much louder. I was certain I had opened a door to a server room. As the door shut behind me, I was instructed through the loudspeakers to remove my blind fold.

When I did I indeed found myself inside a large serverhall, row upon row with servers and switches and storage units. Every other row is a hot aisle followed by a cold aisle. The fan noise was unbearably loud. The LED's of all the machines blinked infernally in green and yellow, and here and there even some unwanted and painfully red ones.

P@nm@n spoke again, dramatically in the speakers, he seemed to enjoy it:

"Behold, the servers of the N3v3r!and! May they serve you as well as you serve them!"

To my left, I saw the others in an operator room behind glass doors. They waved to me to join them.

There, safely shielded from both the cold and the sound, I got the introduction to the N3v3r!and backbone of the online resources of the operation. Both on the internet and on the darknet. It was a pretty impressive setup. Like most of the things the Barrie IT and N3v3r!and had built. It was clear that everything was well thought of and carefully constructed. All with a clear purpose and a clean technical solution. Nothing complex. Each component in the entire machinery is well fitted for its purpose. The complexity itself was in the entire setup.

I was told that we were in the basement floor of the office building, a few stories below the garage. And between us and the garage was the London server room of Barrie IT. I found it a bit poetic that the thing most protected and most secret was buried the deepest. Since I was, and still am, a nerd, I had to point out the red LED's. Apparently there had been some sick leave in the past week, but they assured me that there was no real danger, but applauded me for bringing it to their attention.

I was offered an operator's seat to take a first peak at the setup. And again, I was stunned. When most companies and organizations build security, it is mostly focused to prevent unwanted visitors from the outside to come inside the environment, but if you are an employee, the resources on the inside are typically meant for you, thus the inside is fairly open. Of course this was not the case here. The security from the outside was impressive in itself, but it was almost heavier on the inside. Naturally, an organization of hackers tends to be both paranoid and suspicious of each other, not to mention others from outside of the organization that could possibly (not likely) breach through, and if they did, they would be stopped by the internal layer of security, and be closely monitored each step of the way, no matter how good you are.

The security

If you are not comfortable in IT-security terms, think of it like this. Say that the IT-environment would be a bank. Now, the building the bank is located in, has external protection. If this server room was the bank, the external security would consist of a tall fence with barbed wires at the top. The fence itself would be made of titanium thread. And electrified with lethal voltage. But unlike an actual physical fence in the real world, this fence would not be equipped with warning signs. Now, if you, for some reason, would think it would be a good idea to perhaps try to get close to the fence, you would find yourself watched by cameras that cover each inch of the fence, and also the area above it. Now, the cameras would also have military grade night vision. And a squad of highly armed security guards watching the videofeed and instantly reacting to any and all trespassing, hoping you make it through all the automated defenses. Oh, and did I mention that they are allowed to use lethal violence. Which, as it just happens, is what they are trained in for the past 20-something years. Oh, and if you would dare to try to make it past the outer fence, undetected or not, dark or daylight, your movement would trigger strong light that simultaneously activates target seeking weapons. Now, not the friendly kind with rubber bullets, noop, the lethal kind. Should you make it past this, you find yourself in a totally stripped and open area, for about 20 feet before you reach a high concrete wall. Each of the 20 feet would be filled with lazers and infrared beams, enough to track the movement of a mosquito with the precision of 0,1 mm in a 3D grid. Again, you would not go undetected and again be targeted by the automatic and lethal defense system. But let's say you would make it to the wall. The wall is twice as high as whatever you would consider thinkable to climb. And thick enough to withstand any vehicle attack against it. It would probably withstand most hand held rocket launchers as well. Now, through this wall is only one opening, manned with heavy security day and night. But let's say you somehow made it past this wall as well. Now you need to pass two more obstacles before you reach the actual building. Still only available through one entrance. The first obstacle would be a moat. Now, I am no expert on moats, but I believe it would smell bad, have tons of creepy things in it, both living and nasty not so living things. Let's just imagine that whatever you fear in water, it's loaded with just that. And once you have swimmed across the moat, you reach a sureline that takes you directly to a minefield that you need to pass. The mines are so sensitive that even the wings of a butterfly would be enough to set them off. But let's pretend you've made it past this as well. Now you've reached the building of the bank itself. Again, only one door in or out. No windows. Basically a fortress, or a bunker, that can withstand almost any armed assaults, and penetration attempts. Even some light bombardment. Each inch inside is monitored with advanced cameras. In each passage there are armed guards, stationed close enough to see each other just by turning their head in different directions. Each guard will have at least two other guards in sight. And between them there are movable units that patrol designated sections with their dogs. And yes, of course the guards are heavily armed. To their teeth with the latest and most advanced weaponry, along with lethal classics like various knives and knuckle-dusters. Included in the package is the training required to handle each tool to make the most use of it. No expenses spared, just like in Jurassic Park.

Now add the technology securitylayer to this heavy physical arrangement and imagine it as the best available technology today, but about two or three generations more advanced than what you can imagine. About one or two generations more advanced than the top secret government-graded technology. And of course, all available resources are coordinated and connected to a central command unit for maximum efficiency.

As you probably can imagine. The security arrangement is effective for keeping people out of here. But, also, it is effective to keep track of each and every individual inside the bank. And keeps a close tab on each and every piece of business that is taking place inside the building. Nothing gets unnoticed. Heck, you cannot even fart without sensors registering it and it is being logged to your activities inside.

I do not think I need to explain, but I believe you can understand that this is like a wet dream for a hacker. So many layers of security and totally impossible to penetrate, and even if you are authorized and are on the inside, it is just about impossible to do anything unnoticed or harmful to the place, both from the perspective of the dence technology and the cheer manpower.

To add to this, a normal secure site, corporate wize, would have two various supply routes for power and internet connections. And perhaps even redundancy with local power-generators and some kind of wireless fallback system, like satellite link or more modern 5G connection(s). Government security - add a few more in numbers and you are about close. Military grade, totally self sustained. This place, all of the above. And redundant once more.

I just had to ask how they paid for all of this, I mean, even a global corporation that made a ton of money still has a limited amount of money. Now we are talking about an organization that does not even exist in terms of paper trails.

The finances

H0kr jumped off his seat, eager to explain. Turns out to be
brilliantly simple. And the idea wasn't even his own, he stole
it from a book or movie or something like that, I can't
remember. But the principal is brilliant as it is easy. When you
make an economic transaction digitally, you can transfer an
infinite number of decimals to the transaction, whichever
currency you use. Now, using physical money, you are limited
to the actual value of the money you use. If you buy
something for 9.99 and pay 10, you would get 0.01 back, if
there is physical money worth 0.01. If not, it will get rounded
up, and you would lose your 0.01, while the store would gain
it. But, and here is the brilliance in it, the store, and every
company, registers all transactions digitally, leaving the 0.01
as a rounded amount that is automatically included in the
actual transaction. Now, there are a few more steps, but please
try to follow it, because it is truly brilliant. Now imagine
thousands, no millions of millions of transactions at a store,
where each generates an additional 0.01 in income to the
store. Over time this adds up to a lot of money. Which is just
bonus money for the store. But let's take it up a notch. Bank
transactions, within the bank's own system. The same thing as
within a store. The bonus money is directed to the bank
instead. But have you ever thought about how banks exchange
transactions? Or how large global systems in general interact
with each other, take airplane traffic as an example. Various
airlines and airports need to interact and exchange
information with each other digitally. Safe. Secure. Robust.

Surprisingly enough, most vital and widely spread technology runs on old machines and on old code, including old transfer protocols. Hokr just happened to make changes in a lot of the backbone systems, getting access to that 0.01 of transactions and tricking the systems to transfer 10 and register that transfer as 9.99 rounded up to 10, but the receiving system registering it as receiving 9.99, and the 0.01 is directed elsewhere. Brilliant, untraceable. Undetectable. And when crossreferensing the transactions the 9.99 is registered as transferred and received, and the 0.01 has just disappeared from the systems. Applied on millions and millions of transactions every day. It counts up to a pretty large amount of money. Totally in the dark, off the books.

Adding to this, the actual customers pay a large amount of money for various products and services, totally legit and in the books.

Again, impressive setup, leaving nothing to chance. A solid operation through and through.

I got a quick overview of the N3v3r!and operations in gathering information as well as spreading it. To my surprise, which I probably would have anticipated, a great many of the leading conspiracy bloggers and various political resistance movements were part of the N3v3r!and sphere. If they were aware of it or not, I cannot say, but it is definitely part of the information infrastructure and the information flow.

Now, I feel that, even if it is not at all in my defense or changes the outcome in any way, but at this moment, I was honored to be accepted into the N3v3r!and and felt that I, perhaps for the first time in my life, belonged somewhere and that I was in a place where I could actually make a difference in this world and where I and my skills were valuable and valued. That feeling changes one's views significantly. And lowers one's guard completely. In hindsight probably part of their strategy. Again, no excuse, just sharing my experience.

Starting to contribute

It is said that a person that starts in a new company or at a new position has fresh eyes and can contribute with new perspectives the first few weeks, then the person is adapted to "the way things are" and are more likely to adopt that way than to create new ways. In my case, I'd say that the first few weeks sparked ideas that kept me going for months on end.

I contributed to the Barrie IT security infrastructure and improved significantly on a global level, including backdoors to the N3v3r!and infrastructure.

I made several crawlers on the internet and on the darknet to gather information about every thinkable public person and structured it into several databases with various potential usage. Figuring that information can and should be used both to boost and destroy people. Or possibly control them. I also implemented facial recognition software and put taps on various video surveillance systems and of course, all social media flows and private images stored in the cloud. Surprisingly easy to find out who is sleeping with who, and mapping public persons having affairs on the side, gathering proof. And as a compliment to the web crawlers I also implemented AI-functions to monitor conversations in all digital channels along with phone records if the face recognition software showed that there was a possible affair going on. And on request from the 3ld3rs of Sim1 (P@nm@n, H0kr and TB311 - a referens I believe secretly pointing toward the Elders of Sion, an assumed hoax for an organization working for jewish global domination, and come to think of it now, Sim1 would also be a movie reference…) I also added cross reference to police databases worldwide and pulled data on known drugdealers, human trafficing, known prostitutes and pimps. To gather as much dirt on people as possible.

I also created online drop-boxes for secret information that would be transferred to the offline N3v3r!and infrastructure, making it easier to actually gather information. Still requiring human interaction and physically bringing it to the boat, putting it on the information entrance gates, but opening up possibilities for far more data to be gathered by people that did not have physical access at the moment. I also restructured the data indexing and created a tagg infrastructure to make it more easy to search and combine, putting far more practical use into the gathered information. Now, despite the strictly separated infrastructures, it was important to move (not copy) certain data from the online N3v3r!and infrastructure to the offline infrastructure. And only deleting it from the online infrastructure once safely uploaded and indexed on the offline site. Eventually I was allowed to automate information flow from online to offline through a series of strictly monitored datanodes, diodes, only allowing traffic to pass in one direction. It is my philosophy that information security is holy. Even so holy that it is allowed to affect user friendliness. But when you can make information flow super secure and user friendly, you should.

Let's just say that, not to brag (or maybe a little), my contribution increased the gathering of useful data, to both the online and offline infrastructures hundred fold. Giving the N3v3r!and far more leverage in its work to bring the corrupt people down, and supporting the right people to come forward. N3v3r!and transformed into a greater force. It transformed from something that had previously been feared and respected to a significant and unmatched player in every imaginable arena.

The energy within the organization was changed from patriotic to invincible. We created a powerful war-machine. And prepared for war on a large scale. It was time to bring down the existing world order and create the new. But not in one go with a big bang, but by slowly making the transaction, unnoticed to the common people, but taking power from the shadows and putting it in the hands of N3v3r!and.

Now, while I was doing all this work and contributed to the new weaponry arsenal, I had the time of my life, and as I said earlier, Bella was a big part of it. Oh, sweet Bella! This is the last contribution of hers to this story. But not the last time I mention her. She had accepted me just the way I was and I could open up to her in ways I had never been able to do to anyone else before. No secrets. And one day she brought me a gift. A set of three books from an Art Books. Three volumes of strange books. The first with just about blank pages, the second with numbered pages, and the third with odd content.

She had heard that it contained some kind of hidden code, and figured that if anyone would be able to find it, it would be me.

Despite my vast experience in tracking down information, I could not find anything online in regards to the identity of Art Books, nor how to crack the code, but I did crack it, eventually. It was when working on those books I got back to the mindset of looking at things as they are, when I have them right in front of me. See them in various perspectives. Like Groll says: "there is always more than meets the eye" and like Roy Hicks and the Wizard discussed - truth is a perspective (if you have not discovered them yet, look 'em up!).

I found this to be very true, and over time, this is the puzzle I built from various tiny pieces, found here and there inside the Barrie IT infrastructure and in the online and offline versions of the N3v3r!and infrastructures.

The implications of it are so great that I needed to keep this information to myself at all times, not sharing it with anyone, especially not my Bella. I hope you are well and unharmed somewhere out there! I miss you!

One last thing I should mention, before I continue, is one of my latest tasks that I was assigned before I discovered the truth. While my contribution had managed to gather and connect evidence from a lot of different sources, storing them centrally and connecting the dots to indisputable proof, I was tasked with building a function to reverse the process and pin point and destroy any evidence at the source, after securing it and storing it in the safe environment of the N3v3r!and infrastructure. It was called a failsafe that only the 3ld3rs would have access to, and that needed the approval of all three to be activated.

Now, I did not finish this tool, but I started it and got it working in theory, and all the code was left behind, so I figure that the tool has been completed and implemented, ready to use at their will.

The yin and yang of the world

As you might have caught from what you've already read so far, there is a hidden layer of power in the shadows. Real power, real money, big money, pulling strings in the visible world, making sure that the visible world is kept in check, and keeping the general public, the masses of people, controllable. The tools are a great many, spanning from politics to corporations, food and health. big pharma, the beauty industry, entertainment, gambling, transport and logistics, digital infrastructure, banks, money transactions, travels, heck even your self image and what you fear… all in the hands of the people in the shadows. All controlled by the geniously designed economic system that our entire world is a slave to.

Now, don't get me wrong, it's not like conspiracy theories where a few people, like the Rothschild-family or the Illuminati, are in control. It is a network and a well kept balance of people operating in the shadows, always looking out for their own interests. Individuals and stakeholders vary over time, but the power of the shadow world is always intact.

All these people and the stakeholders are, just so happened, active clients of Barrie IT. Along with many world leading cooperatives and governing functions. Now what separates the shadow people from the others is client status within Barrie IT. Remember those I spoke to about passwords on my first part of the initiation? Well, that's the client segment. The

119

VIP-clients. Those with real power. They are also the prime targets of the offline databases of the N3v3r!and. Not the only targets, but the primary targets.

With Barrie IT being an official (or through front companies) security partner to the VIP segment, and various other global and prominent establishments, N3v3r!and got access to a lot of information that they would not easily obtain through standard methods of hacking or espionage. Leaving them with exclusive rights to their very own covert goldmine.

By secretly connecting to those VIP-clients and mapping them, collecting dirt and useful information on them, N3v3r!and cleverly position themselves as the opposite pole, and, oddly enough also working as a unifying force, providing platforms and forums for the people in the shadows to meet, talk, decide, without being out in the open, keeping well within the shadows.

The shadow people are the black in the Yin and Yang sign, and N3v3r!and are the white. Or at least that is what I thought. I learned that the balance in the Yin and Yang is the good, and the unbalance of Yin and Yang is the bad. Not as I thought that the white being good and black being bad. Which gives an entirely new meaning to it all. At least for me.

Now, the perspective that N3v3r!and sells to their members is that the mission of the entire operation is to be an opposite force to the shadow people. To bring that force down, let the new world order rise in the aches of the shadows. Letting the truth out. And until that is doable, acting as a force to minimize the damage the people in the shadow inflict on this world. And keeping them in check so they cannot do whatever they want.

When joining the N3v3r!and I thought the strategy to join with the enemy and engage in their cause was a bit odd, but at the same time, I could see some logic to it, since it gave the N3v3r!and a totally unique position to act as a true player in the game. Sleep with the enemy so to speak. But something still felt wrong. You don't join the devil's forces if you want to fight the devil. Not even guerilla warriors join or infiltrate the army they want to fight.

Not yin and yang, opposite sides of the same coin

(or Fading - to use the Muddhedd song)

As I worked on the information structure, adding tags and joining more and more sources, I could look at the information from new perspectives. At first I saw it as strange coincidences, but when one incident became two, and two seemed to multiply and then rapidly spreading to various aspects of type of information, contaminating economic transactions, communications, geotags, traces of covering tracks of various events in order to hide things, all my warning flags raised.

What slowly emerged as patterns throughout the structured information was a terrifying fact. The N3v3r!and is not a counterpart to the people in the shadow, it is a part of it. Different sides of the same coin. Different tools to obtain the same goal.

If this is a war, then the people in the shadows are commanding the forces on both sides, feeding the war and keeping gaining from it. Keep gaining money, keep gaining control, keep gaining secrecy. Keeping both sides in the conflict occupied with the conflict. Training both sides, or rather all sides, to fight the others, providing more efficient strategies, tools and weaponry. But only enough to maintain the balance and maintain all people in the machinery occupied enough to not start asking the right questions or seeing things as they are. All to cover their existence and keep staying concealed in the eye of the hurricane.

This is a complex war with multiple fronts, and all the fronts are controlled and maintained by central management. The 3ld3rs are part of the governing apparatus. With its equivalent on "the other side" (or perhaps sides). A high stake game of players playing players. Brilliantly managed. And as new battlefronts appear from uncontrolled groups, they are methodically infiltrated and included in the ongoing all-on-all war.

I realized that the truth had been with me from the start, before I found the N3v3r!and. It was right there at the Eiffel Tower. Truth is !free. It is not, but I wanted to believe that it was not set free and that the N3v3r!and would help in doing so. Now I've seen it from a different perspective. Truth is not free, as in it having a price. Not just a small price. But large numbers. On a global scale. And I've just helped out to reinforce its position and increased the price tag significantly. Yay! Well done me! Not! But I cannot undo it. Not even I thought about building in backdoors for myself to use in case of emergency. I never thought that it would be needed. Alas, I was wrong. So, so wrong.

And this was not the game to play to set the truth free. That game is completely different, and the arena is not where I thought it would be.

Part III

Fighting N3v3r!and

After Darkness (Muddhedd)

Now, it is possible that you share my view of the N3v3r!and and that they have become something other than what they intended from the start. They have become the thing that they tried to prevent, and not only that, they have become the most important tool into keeping things as they are. This is nothing I can support, and even if I do realize the irony in dividing the N3v3r!and into them and they, creating an opposite from me, we and us, I still oppose *them. They* are my enemy.

Naturally, I can only see one possible way forward. I need to fight N3v3r!and and see it destroyed, along with all its governing parts. The whole establishment needs to be torn apart. I need to bring the storm to the center of itself, and blind the eye of the hurricane.

Knowing the truth behind it, and knowing that the truth is a perspective, I also realize that I am one individual among many billions. There is not much one person can do, especially not while the big mass is still trapped in the global game that they are playing, by rules they have created.

I cannot fight them alone. I need you to wake up. I need you to fight them as well, as an individual, where you reclaim your free will, where you take responsibility for your choices and choose to live an active life.

I will do everything in my power to keep waking people up, unplug people from the matrix, if you will. And I will continue to crawl the web, but this war will not be fought in a conventional way, this war will be fought in the minds of every single human soul in this world. It is not a physical war, it is a war of information, disinformation and about keeping everybody in check and controllable.

You are both the victim, the collateral damage, the soldier and the scene of the war. This is a war with emotional bloodspill. Where casualties are not counted in dead bodies but in free minds, uncontrollable. Open minds practicing free will.

This is your fight. And believe it or not, your fight is not with them. It is with you. An internal struggle that each and every one of us needs to win in order to be free of their control and crush them once and for all.

To me, the foundation of this world needs to be recreated. I can only see this happening with new guidelines, accepted by a united front of world citizens.

My fight has begun. Perhaps I have convinced you to join me. If so, this is my short manifesto, my vision of a sustainable future with truly free individuals.

It is divided into three parts for each person and four pillars for society.

What we all need to accept

- Truth is a perspective - your truth might not be the truth of another, and other truths may not be true to you, but we all need to respect each other no matter what truth we follow.
- Each truth needs to be able to be questioned, if it is too weak to be questioned it is dangerous and needs to be abandoned.
- This world is not just, fair nor equal. But we all have the same responsibilities and rights. No person is of greater value than any other. We are just different. And we all need to accept and embrace our differences and see them for what they really are; our strength. All different pieces in a complex machinery where each part cannot work without all the other parts and where the entire machinery is dependent on all parts. We need to see past our differences and look out for each other by including and accepting rather than excluding and dividing.
- There is no they, only we.
- We all need to accept the direct democratic system and let go of the old so called democracy. The true will of the many needs to be governing.
- We need to remember the past, all versions, to avoid history repeating itself.
- Respect each individual as an individual, regardless of sex, sexual orientation, skincolor, origin, nationality, religious belief or place in the social structure.

- Leave judging to courts and the legal pillar of society.

Individual responsibilities

- When meeting another person you have three choices:
  - Love
  - Respect
  - Accept

  In order for others to at least accept you as you are, and your thoughts and opinions, you need to at least accept the other person. Respect those who deserve it, and love those closest to you.

  Hate and exclusion is never an option, since it divides people into different and opposite polarities.
- When meeting another's opinion or thoughts you need to question it and look at it from different angles, while simultaneously having your own opinion or thoughts questioned and examined. Only strong positions that survive questioning are worth keeping and clinging on to. The choices you have here are:
  - Adopt
  - Respect
  - Accept

  It is never up to you to convince another to change their opinion or thoughts, it is always the individual's responsibility.
- When taking part of information, always check the source and factor in the purpose of the information,

from the perspective of the source. It may be true from that perspective, but you do not need to share that perspective. Truth is always a perspective. Choose your perspective and honor it as well as others.

- Take part in the global community and voice your thoughts and opinion and use your right to vote.
- Accept the decision of the majority, even if you feel like you never share the opinion of the majority, it is not a human right to get the way you want it to be, but it is your responsibility to help shape what will be.
- Develop and challenge yourself to be the best version of yourself that you can be. You are unique and important to this world as you are, and owe the world your best. Fully aware that your best today might not be the same as yesterday. You are a human being, not a robot!
- You need to contribute to society, at least by paying tax. Other commitments are voluntary.

Individual rights

- You have the right to be who you are, believe in a religion or not, think and express whatever you want, as long as you are prepared to have your thoughts or beliefs challenged by others.

- You have the right to your worth as a free human being, as long as you obey the laws created by society. If not, you forfeit your rights and freedom.
- You have the right to own property and things, and if you choose to, you are fully responsible for all your belongings as long as they are in your possession.
- You have the right to your own choices, as long as they do not conflict with the laws of society.
- You have the right to vote in direct democratic elections and day to day operations.
- You have the right to privacy, unless it conflicts with the laws of society.

The structure of society is built on four founding pillars

1. Direct democracy

The old coalitions of political parties are obsolete. It is a way of creating polarity, us versus them. Even in democracy where there are several parties to choose from it is still a limited choice and the different parties represent partially ideas or ideologies, but not enough to be pure, but still too much to be able to make compromises that will represent the voting population as a whole, often they end up looking out for themselves and represent a political view and solution that will keep them in power for as long as possible. And those not in power will represent politics to get them elected.

Direct democracy on the other hand removes the power from the politicians and puts it right back in the voting population's hands. The politicians of direct democracy are sources of information and perspective. The real power lies with the people, and each vote in the democratic chamber is the votes of the people. Each question that is up for decision is also votable for each and every individual. It is up to the politicians to raise public awareness and get people to commit to vote.

This way, different politicians can form temporary coalitions in different questions and push for the most sustainable collaboration for each question. And as for the voters, it is easier to voice your own opinion, question by question, instead of choosing a package where most questions suit you.

Sure enough, it is hard to get voters in the general public to commit to actively making choices in day-to-day political processes, but the positive outcome of actually being able to influence one's daily life will raise awareness and commitment over time. It's always the will of the majority that decides. Even if the vote count is low.

This system makes it harder for groups or companies to get their will through, as the control of everything is in the hands of each and every person.

2. Freedom of information

Today we live in a world filled with information and disinformation. Facts and rumors. Truth. Lies. Heroes and villains. We have forgotten that there is always perspective on things. One mans freedomfighter is another mans terrorist. Nothing in this world is black or white, there is the entire gray-scale in between, but it does not stop there, because we have all the colors and colors in various shades. Countless possibilities. Life just hates binary. It is extremely rare that it is either black or white.

Freedom of information is a two-edged sword. Anybody can share any information, true or false, it is within each individual's rights, which at the same time puts a great responsibility on you as a consumer of information. You need to assign a credibility value to each and every piece of information that you consume. Based on the source, the intention of the information from the source and other factors that you already know, making the information you consume either credible or not. Credible information you can relay to others and use as the base of further steps, and when you deem information unworthy it needs to be discarded.

Remember, your opinion of the information is only your opinion, it is not a fact that others need to obey. Other people can, and most probably will draw different conclusions from the same information, which is as it should.

Today we have trusted sources, such as newspapers, universities, companies etc. They are to be considered information brokers. Any information broker should be considered biased based on their goals. Don't let any scourse ever be unquestioned and any piece of information accepted on autopilot.

3. Law and order

Society dictates laws, society is responsible to uphold the law. The law is dictated by Direct Democracy by the majority. In this pillar of society you have obligations, use your right to vote to be a part of shaping the laws of society, and as a world citizen, accept and obey the laws of society. You also have obligations to other citizens. You take care of your relationship with the law, and leave everybody else to handle their relationship with the law. Unless you are employed by the law, you leave it up to the law to handle the responsibility to uphold it. There is absolutely no reason to interfere in other people's business, with one exception. If you or someone close to you are on the receiving end of a crime, being, or see a risk of being a crime victim. Then you should act, preferably in advance if possible, and report the transgression towards you to the law and let the law handle it.

4. Collective responsibility

In this new world order, there is no they or them, only we and us. You are a part of this community. This gives you rights within the society, but you are also a part of the society and leaves you with a responsibility towards the society, other living beings and this planet. If you ever think that someone else needs to fix something, you are wrong, it is you that needs to fix it, and if you cannot, you need to raise awareness at the right place. If you find trash on the street it may not be your duty to pick it up and place it where it belongs, there might be someone hired to do just that task, but if you do not wish your city, neighborhood or area to have trash laying around on the ground, you can either pick it up or leave it and accept that your neighborhood is dirty.

This is a typical thing you can fix yourself with minimum effort, and if we all share this responsibility, we will all be rewarded with a clean and neat city. This is a responsibility you can, and should take as a part of society. And if you see a broken streetlight, that is not something you can fix for yourself, but you can make sure to report it to the appropriate authorities so it can be fixed. That is your responsibility if you see it, do not expect someone else to do it. If you see something it is your responsibility to act. If not, you are part of the problem with your inaction.

There is a terrible event that describes this perfectly.

In a cityarea, in an alley with several windows and a few balconies, a woman was raped by a man. She screamed for help, and a lot of people heard it, and lights went on in several windows, and people looked out to see what the fuss was about. This scared away the man. But the woman was hurt and in shock and could not leave the place, so the man returned a second time to continue his assault. Of course the woman screamed again. Same thing repeated once more, lights went on in several windows, people were looking out to see what the fuss was about, someone even opened the window yelling to the man to stop. Once more he was scared away and the poor woman still lay raped, bruiced and half beaten to death. But as the man had left, the noises stopped and people went back to sleep once more. But the man returned a third time, and then finished what he had started, leaving the poor woman dead.

When the police eventually were notified and interrogated all the neighbors with windows facing the alley, almost everybody reported that they had heard what was going on, seen it, understood that the woman had been attacked, but believed that it was not their business and expected someone else to call the police. Perhaps, if someone had called the police at once, the poor woman might not have had to die.

The perspective here is that there is not someone else, there is only you, and your responsibility to act. Whatever the situation might be.

Respect our one world, and all living beings in it. We are dependent on our world, it is not in any way dependent on us.

And some final words about the economy.

Even if what I have specified above is a utopia, you can act today. And the strongest weapon you have in your arenal when you wake up is your money. How you choose to spend it is your way of turning the tides. If you stop supporting a company with your money, and more follow you, they will eventually vanish.

If you choose to listen to commercials and keep buying things they say you need, it will keep you occupied and in their power.

When you wake up and choose to focus on the things that matter to you, the way it matters to you and how you would like it to be, then they lose control over you.

The more in debt you are, the more controllable you are.

The more things you think you need to buy and the more things you think you need to do, the more control they have on you. And the more control they have on you, the more they will dictate what you need to buy and do.

Go back to the core of you, find your own happiness, not through spending money but simply by being. Do only things that matter to you. That enriches your life. Own only things that matter to you and enrich your life. Spend money only on things and experiences that matter to you and that enriches your life.

Coming full circle

(or Wild Oak - to use the Muddhedd song title)

Now, as promised, I will end where I started.

You need to wake up. It is time! You need to find and follow your white rabbit!